adibas

adibas

Zaza Burchuladze

Translated by
Guram Sanikidze

DALKEY ARCHIVE PRESS
CHAMPAIGN / LONDON / DUBLIN

Originally published in Georgian as *adibas* by
Bakur Sulakauri Publishing, 2010

Library of Congress Cataloging-in-Publication Data

Burculaze, Zaza.
Adibas / Zaza Burchuladze ; translated by Guram Sanikidze. -- First edition.
pages cm
ISBN 978-1-56478-925-9 (acid-free paper)
I. Sanikidze, Guram, translator. II. Title.
PK9169.B87A6513 2014
899'.969--dc23
2013040515

Partially funded by a grant from the Illinois Arts Council, a state agency

Georgian Literature Series is published thanks to the support of the
Ministry of Culture and Monument Protection of Georgia.

www.dalkeyarchive.com

Cover: design and composition by Mikhail Iliatov
Cover image: *Bisque Doll*, Florian Lehmuth, 2012

Printed on permanent/durable acid-free paper

TABLE OF CONTENTS

adibas:

1. fake adidas

2. surrogate, or imitation in general

3. any fake or falsified thing, situation, fact, etc.

1. MORNING MULTIMEDIA

Bobo can do anything. She cooks pasta fabulously, has seen all the seasons of *Lost*, and drives me crazy the way she sucks; she does it elaborately, with great care.

Bobo. At the bare mention of the name, her firm nipples, cream-rubbed body, slender waistline, and dexterous tongue loom before my eyes. I lie in bed alone. My cell phone shows it's half past nine; I slept two hours longer than usual. All I remember from my dream is that my brain was lit up like a light bulb and colored sparks raced through its convolutions, the way signals flash through a fiber-optic cable.

A glass of pasteurized milk is on the nightstand by my bed; a plate containing a Centrum pill and a croissant are next to the glass. I figure that this is going to become my morning regimen in the near future. Was I really out so cold that I couldn't hear Bobo get up, get dressed, and run down for the croissant?

As soon as I reach for the croissant, Aphex jumps up onto the bed, wagging his tail right and left, so that my image of him is blurred. He licks my face too, trying to stick his warm, wet tongue through my lips, a sort of "long time, no see." I already know the strategic way he fakes affection. All he wants from me is the croissant. He lies down on my chest, looking fawningly into my eyes.

"Fuck off," I say. "Now!"

He turns away dismally, head down, his tail between his legs, and sits on Bobo's pillow looking fixedly at the croissant. He's got really big, watery eyes, just like Amélie from the movie *Amélie*. He wants to snatch the croissant from my hand, but doesn't dare. I feel for him. This croissant is the best in Tbilisi, baked in the newly opened bakery on the ground floor of the building I live in. They put cherry jam, raisins, marzipan, chocolate, or farmer's cheese inside—they're more than just croissants, they're the *Goldberg Variations* as performed by Glenn Gould.

Aphex looks hard into my eyes, trying to soften me up. To no avail, though. His begging doesn't work today. We both know that he can't fool me and he won't get a crumb. The airy-soft bakery dough melts in my mouth, sliding down and warming the inside of my belly.

I take off the blanket and look at my bloodshot cock; it lies on my stomach, swelling up in a funny sort of way. I feel it throbbing, and can't take my eyes off it. "My Funny Valentine"—that's what Bobo named it. There's something hypnotic about a hardon. Are stomach and cock all that really matter? Undoubtedly. Even Aphex gets it: he shifts his gaze between the two. I hold the croissant in one hand, My Funny Valentine in the other.

I swallow the Centrum pill, drinking it down with the milk. Then I run to the bathroom. Aphex, sore as hell that he didn't get the croissant, goes after me barking, sort of nipping at my heel. The plasma screen is on in the living room. TV1000 is showing *Pan's Labyrinth.* Trying to show, that is. The frame's stuck. The white monster puts its eye-encrusted palms to its face, but half the frame is pixelated. *No signal to display* pops up on the screen. This cable TV has really been fucking up recently. I flip the channel to Imedi. A tank column rattles along some highway. A rapid-fire voice-over says: ". . . General Kulakhmetov strongly denies that Russian tanks have entered Tbilisi, calling reports 'misinformed.' Nevertheless, high-intensity shooting has been heard for as long as one hour in Didi Digomi . . ."

First thing I do is get into a hot shower, thoroughly massaging myself with a granular, coconut flake body scrub. I turn the water down to icy-cold and brush my teeth in my own special way. The two things I'll never give up are cold showers in the morning and brushing my teeth until my gums start bleeding. The hard is still on. Thanks to the sweetish odor of the body scrub, Bobo comes back to me again. I don't give a damn that she won't swallow cum; even now I would gladly cum in her mouth.

I separate women into two categories: the ones who swallow and the ones who keep cum in their mouths. I can tell from experience that the latter blow better than the former. Of course, this isn't a law of nature in any way. I just know it from experience. Take Bobo. She doesn't swallow, but her blow jobs are heavenly. When I shoot, her mouth fills up with cum while she prays in her heart. That's what I call a true blow job, a saintly practice: cum in mouth, prayer in heart, and cock in hand.

I picked up Bobo the day before yesterday at a party in Tsavkisi. It was at the summer house of a mutual acquaintance—a night of black candles, lousy ecstasy, boozy delirium, and the alchemy of love. Since then, I've learned that Bobo is a straightforward person, preferring black clothes and plain talk. Her Skype handle is *alien_style*, she has a pierced navel (a tiny platinum embryo), and she loves electronic music. She's got a firm body, high tits, and a tight ass. However, there's something vamp-like about her; she's more sexy than pretty.

She was standing alone by the sound system, sipping Red Bull through a straw. I pushed through a crowd of dancers rolling on ecstasy and got over to the speakers, where I *accidentally* bumped into her.

"Sorry!" I shouted.

The way she smiled, I realized she hadn't heard me. Small wonder though; I couldn't even hear myself through the booming bass.

"Borena!" she shouted back.

I thought she was kidding. "Borena?"

She nodded. "Or just Bobo."

After we tried and failed to dance to the beat of the music, we ended up as if by magic in the next room where, jaws askew, we made out zealously for a long time. As though in a trance, I figured we could fuck right there on the sofa. Later, we exchanged tunes on our cell phones using Bluetooth, laughed a lot over whatever bullshit, and bitched about everyone and everything. Finally we cuddled up and fell asleep right there, just like in a TV series; the camera pans out, romantic music comes on, and credits appear on the screen.

I figure that everything is coming together on its own. Bobo's going to enter my life once and for all, just like a complete renovation transforming a shabby apartment. I, for one, am willing to accept all that she's going to bring into my life: Johnny Depp movies, Centrum, a Darth Vader poster, and mild hysterics before her periods.

I put on a bathrobe. Aphex lifts his rear leg for me to see, defiantly pees on the fridge, and then runs far away to safety. That's the shitty way he pays me back. Happy about what he's done, he can hardly wait to see my reaction. Well, he can wait till the cows come home. The bastard is nervous and stiff all over, just like Antonio Gades before a performance, waiting for me to shout an order to dance flamenco. I pretend nothing's the matter and coolly wipe up his pee with napkins. I just wonder if all Chihuahuas terrorize their masters like this, or if Aphex is spoiled rotten. Out of the corner of my eye, I see him watching me in amazement; he realizes that the game is up.

I open the fridge. As soon as the inner light goes on, it dawns on me that in my dream my head was lit with the exact same brightness. Not like cocaine, when you take it through the nose and it fires your brain up like hell. It was a demure bulb, fit for a good old lampshade in any sweet grandma's bedroom.

The TV plays in the living room: ". . . the motorized rifle battalion of the 42nd division is heading downtown along the right embankment of the Mtkvari River. The battalion includes eighty units of heavy machinery and thirty tanks . . ."

A paperback book and Bobo's open laptop are on the kitchen table by the window. The laptop vibrates lightly, shaking the table. I see the book for the first time ever; there's a silhouette on the cover:

Gone with the Balloon.

Seems like a contemporary novel—could be horror or something postmodern.

First thing I do is click on YouTube, searching for whatever crap. I download a video of Cannibal Corpse, hoping George Fisher's raucousness will soften my hard-on. I sit down in a chair, lift the hem of my bathrobe, stare at my stiff cock, and think about Bobo. It's hard to have a hard-on and not think of Bobo, or, rather, to think of Bobo and not get a hard-on. The Cannibals fail to make me go soft. Fisher wheezes: *Draining the snot, I rip out the eyeees* . . . and rotates his head propeller-like, his long, loose hair waving about.

I give Bobo a buzz, all to no avail. *Your mobile phone is blocked or out of coverage.* Where could she have gone? I look through the open window. A herd of bicyclists rides along the highway. They look tired, bending forward in their seats and pushing the pedals heavily. Due to their egg-shaped helmets, reflective glasses, and aerodynamic suits—which stick to their bodies—they look like aliens. A gray Ford Sierra drives behind the herd.

I snuggle up in my chair and take a photo of my cock with my cell phone. Then I check the quality of the photo on the screen and assure myself one more time that three megapixels can't approximate the real-life image. I still text it to Bobo. A winged envelope flies away on the screen: *message sent to Bobo.*

2. TOY TRIANGLES

"Two mojitos," I tell the bartender.

His name is Paata. Everyone calls him Bob, though. It's a Bob Marley thing. I never call him that, by the way. His fake reggae style gets on my nerves. A marijuana-colored shirt, Jamaican dreads, leather beads, and loose shorts give the basic picture of him. Bob nods quickly and smiles at me slyly. I hate to be checked out in such an obvious way. While he slices a lime and crushes ice, I walk over to a plastic chair under an umbrella and seat myself.

The Vake Swimming Pool bustles with the silicon-breasted widows of mobsters, businessmen's wives with cellulite-heavy waists, cum-eating Barbie girls in huge sunglasses, gay ravers with pierced navels, mama's boys with all their dreams coming true, and dozens of young, firm bodies just ready to be sent to the Eurovision Song Contest. The smells of water, cosmetics, fresh chlorine, and disinfectant mix together. The water in the pool dazzles and blinds; neutral music pours out from the sound system. You can't love music like that. But it can't get at you, either. You two, you exist separately. I suspect this kind of music is specifically composed to be played in the spas and elevators of luxury hotels. You never know when it starts or ends. It's not yet ten A.M. and the sun is sizzling nastily. Nobody is swimming though. Sapped by the heat and white as sheets, Tbilisians lounge under umbrellas, in pool chairs. All you're supposed to do here is just bake beside the swimming pool; swimming itself is not looked upon with favor.

With her chocolate-colored skin, Tako stands out. She's barefooted at the edge of the pool, her eyes closed and her back to me. Her bathing suit, V-shaped panties and tiny triangles tied with thread and which cover almost nothing, can barely be made out.

These geometric shapes merge with her suntan so well, you can hardly see them on her body. Even her tattoo is hidden by the suntan. (By the way, she got a small target tattooed on the nape of her neck just two weeks earlier.)

Tako got that tattoo in such an unfashionable spot for the simple reason that next to her clitoris, her nape is her most sensitive erogenous zone, a sort of external G-spot. But she seems to have gone too far, kind of like a teenage girl who protests against everything and declares her own parents her bitterest enemies, and so ends up masturbating frequently and making reckless decisions. But how could I tell her all that, anyway?

By the way, a couple weeks ago I almost showed some trashy tendencies, too. I mean that I came very close to getting a tattoo on some part of my body. You know, I'd always felt like having a big Avatar-like arrow inked onto my shaved head, starting at the nape of my neck and extending all the way over my head and down to the place where my eyebrows meet. I'd have had my body tattooed all over long ago, just like some yakuza, but the fact that all that lasts forever annoys the hell out of me. While the tattoo artist was working on Tako's neck, I sat in a leather armchair and looked through his catalogues. The range seemed to include almost everything from Aztec/Incan images to bar codes to SS symbols to pictures of Che. There were mottled ones, looking like CAT scans, and monochrome ones, like amateurish stencils. You could find funny ones as well. Like, a Dao monad, the standard yin and yang symbol, and *der grüne punkt* intertwined in just one tattoo.

I also liked one of the god of war, Huitzilopochtli, who was depicted as a hummingbird armed to the teeth and dressed in knight's armor. It looked like Bumblebee transforming from a Chevrolet Camaro into an iron giant. Then I checked it out on Wikipedia and learned that in ancient times, people were even offered up as sacrifices to this tiny little bird. Well, if I were sure that I'd be understood correctly, I'd gladly sacrifice half of Tbilisi to some bird. Even a chicken would do just as well.

I find that I am not alone by the bar. A couple sits at a plastic table with their glasses half-filled with some juice. A pack of Vogues are also on the table, with a lighter inside. The woman is sitting in such a way that all I can see are her fragile shoulders, her thin arm lying on the table, and the heel of her foot under the chair. There's a piece of yellowed, warped, and scaly skin on her heel. She is whispering something into the man's ear, her body bent slightly forward. The man nods now and again, typing a message on his phone.

I have no idea why I suddenly recollect in detail the dream I had that morning. In the dream, I was in Shevardnadze's Krtsanisi residence, interviewing him. He was wearing normal, ordinary clothes, a blue suit and a sky-blue shirt, but on his feet he wore plush, rosy slippers with rabbit ears. We were sitting in chairs at a low table with a bottle of Borjomi mineral water and two glasses. I was holding a voice recorder in my hand for some reason. The chair leather and Shevardnadze's skin were the same color. I couldn't tell where Shevardnadze finished and the chair began. He reminded me of the Big Lebowski from the movie *The Big Lebowski*. He wouldn't move his lips. Just like a clockwork puppet, sounds seemed to ooze out of his mouth. Sedately, he recollected: ". . . once when I was secretary general, I visited the filmmaker Parajanov in his small half-wooden house in Mtatsminda. He was very happy to see me and a little worried at the same time, because as he told me in his own words, he had nothing to treat me to. He excused himself and said he would drop by his neighbor's for a minute to get some food. I stopped him, saying that if I needed food, I would have brought some along myself. He kept plenty of strange things in those rooms of his; it was just like a museum. Later I moved to Moscow. The Armenians, however, moved the house to Yerevan in secrecy. Yes, everything that belonged to Parajanov's house they managed to move away piece by piece, eventually opening a wonderful museum in Yerevan. Sometime later I put them to shame, but they defied me, saying that Parajanov was Armenian just like them, and that they were not ashamed one bit."

The flashback of the dream vanishes. Tako has a small set of earphones stuck in her ears. She's holding an iPod, its white cord looking even whiter against the background of her suntan than it really is. Just like a milky stripe in a bar of chocolate. She looks as if she cares about no one, as if she's alone with herself, *in herself*. Like a cobra ready to strike, she gently sways to and fro to the beat of her music. She is aware, however, that she's disturbing the sluggish day-to-day of the pool, and that everybody is watching her closely but surreptitiously, with artificial nonchalance. Watching outright is unacceptable in this arena. However, peeping in secrecy makes the watching more erotic that with any porno. And this is more than just a show. This is a magic show: a sawing illusion. And that's just what Tako wants. She wants to be like the woman who is about to lie inside a box and get sawed in half in front of an audience. She wants everyone to watch her and get hard-ons. Why not? I love everything she does. I like myself when I see the way Tako gives them hard-ons. I get a hard-on myself, watching her firm boobs, her tight ass, her slightly broad, boy-like shoulders . . .

"Two mojitos." Bob puts the glasses on the counter.

The water sparkles in the pool like the result of some special effect. And it vibrates as if it's being shaken. A growing drone all of a sudden reaches its peak and then dies away as fast as it started. A fighter jet flies so low that its breeze and shadow pass over the pool. The umbrellas near the bar quiver heavily; the water in the pool wobbles. Relaxed Tbilisians lounge in their pool chairs. Everyone pretends nothing is up. Only one skinny woman bends sideways and looks up at the sky.

As soon as I start sipping the mojito, I wish I had just gotten still water. It's mixed with vodka rather than Bacardi. Even spearmint can't kill the sickening taste of alcohol. Feeling a little woozy from the heat, I creep up on Tako and kiss her sun-warmed nape. It makes her shiver right away. I taste bittersweet tanning cream on my lips. My brain sends a signal down to my cock. Right away I feel my sphincter contracting, a light electric shock going through my balls. In cases like this, it's my sphincter that contracts first. Then my balls twitch. But I don't have a hard-on yet. Jazz music filters vaguely through her earphones. My thoughts are getting all muddled—I can't understand why Tako is listening to jazz. I kiss her nape again, waiting in vain for the electronic remix to take over.

Tako turns to me. Smiling, she opens her eyes slightly. The sparkling water dazzles her eyes. I hand her a mojito and ask with a hand gesture what she's listening to. In reply, she points to her iPod screen. I can't see anything, though. The screen reflects the sunshine. Tako sways again like a dancing cobra. Before she takes away her hand, I catch sight of her index fingernail. The polish is off in one place.

3. DIPLOMAT IN ATTACHÉ CASE

I lounge on the bench outside an empty bus stop across from the city concert hall, a newsstand beside me. An *Alia* headline in large type catches my eye: DIPLOMAT IN DIPLOMAT'S ATTACHÉ CASE. The newsman's shadow is seen through the open door. A Zhiguli taxi is parked at the curb, the driver's door open. The driver leans back in his chair, a wet handkerchief on his forehead. A tiny guy, keeping his knees together girl-like. The voice of a newscaster plays from the speakers: ". . . Russian army units are heading along the right embankment of the Mtkvari River. Roadblocks are laid out on Beijing Street, by the Sports Palace, and by Public Broadcaster . . ."

The Zhiguli reminds me of the taxi drivers in Telavi—nice, considerate guys. Not a chance they would utter a word until spoken to. Most of them have perfectly round bellies, as if they had just gulped down great big watermelons, and they sit at the wheels of their silver-colored Opel Vectras in a sort of ultra-dignified Kakhetian way, so that you feel shy just getting in. In Telavi, by the way, you can't find any other taxi model. I'd really like to paint an Opel logo up in the corner of the Kakheti coat of arms. Telavi is a provincial town alive with wine, watermelons, potted cacti (available all over the place, for some unknown reason), and silvery Opel Vectras. You can hardly hold your tears back when, looking inside those cars, you find neatly arranged cassettes that ring forgotten bells: TDK, AGFA, BASF, MAXELL, DENON. Those tapes make you sort of nostalgic and sorry at the same time. Both cassettes and cockroaches vanished into thin air at some stage of my life.

At the entrance to Vera Park I catch sight of a street sweeper.

He has a thick black bush of hair and a big mustache. In a funny sort of way, he bears a resemblance to Benicio del Toro in the role of Dr. Gonzo. The LSD I took yesterday reminds me of itself. Some object circles over the Chess Palace in the same geometric way as a fly under a ceiling lamp. I just can't make out whether the object is a surveillance drone or a seagull. Despite being annoyed by the voice of the newscaster, I still stand in between the newsstand and the Zhiguli. The object is best seen from there. After a moment it seems to "spot" me, raises itself, takes a sharp nosedive, and disappears through the tress.

". . . a short time ago, Russian military boats started patrolling the Mtkvari River from Mtskheta to Gardabani . . ." comes from the taxi.

After a while, the surveillance drone reappears from behind the Chess Palace, watches me for a minute, and then slowly starts flying toward me. The identified flying object. Eventually, it gets so close that I can make out my own reflection through the objective lens built into its nose. (РФ)-08 is stamped under a curve bent like a seagull's wing. I stand petrified. It seems to sense that the two of us are soul mates, and starts circling around me, changing its direction now and then as unexpectedly as a 3D clock on a computer screen saver. It makes almost no sound. All I can see are its lenses sliding back and forth along the objective when it starts to zoom. All of a sudden, (РФ)-08 stops in midair, its lenses dilating to the limit, fixing me as the apple of its eye.

"You motherfucker!" comes a voice from behind my back.

I turn around so sharply that a poignant smell of antiperspirant from my own armpit hits my nose. The street sweeper is running toward me, waving his broom menacingly. Instinctively I stagger aside, burying my face in my hands. Even an ordinary broom can turn into a powerful weapon in the wrong hands. I realize too late that the street sweeper doesn't care about me; he strikes at (РФ)-08 with his broom, but only fans the air. The object moves aside with lightning speed. The street sweeper waves his broom as if it were a genuine Jedi lightsaber, but (РФ)-08 is faster. It turns away and flies back toward the Chess Palace. The sweeper swishes the broom threateningly.

"Fuck your ass, anyway," he spits from between his teeth. Then he turns and runs over to me. "You okay, bro?" he asks compassionately, breathing heavily, his eyes glowing with indignation.

He looks even more furious than those Orthodox Christians who, armed with crosses, descended upon vampires at the Halloween party at Club No. 1 last year. He seems out of control, with his angry eyes incredulous and piercing at the same time, like Clint Eastwood's. He comes so close that I can see the hair sticking out of his nostrils. His legs are set far apart from each other, sort of "П"-like; if he crapped his pants, he wouldn't even get shit on his legs. He looks into my eyes intently, as if trying to read something there.

"I'm okay," I comfort him. "I'm really okay."

"Are you sure, man?" He surveys me from head to foot.

"Yeah, I'm sure." Then I repeat it as he looks at me suspiciously. "Yeah, *I'm sure*."

"You've got to get yourself checked." He breathes in deeply. I can't guess what he means. "Sure that motherfucker got you irradiated." He slings his broom over his shoulder.

Got me irradiated? His assumption sounds like a threat, like the Bourne ultimatum from the movie *The Bourne Ultimatum*.

"No," I say. "It had no time at all to do that."

Only now do I catch sight of a small, YouTube window-sized screen built into his stomach, just like the Teletubbies have. The message in one corner of the screen reads: *press here to enter full screen mode.* I press the message. All of a sudden, everything moves backward somehow: the street, the Zhiguli, the street sweeper . . . as if the molecular system of the air has changed and the picture, going into perspective, takes on a sepia effect, becoming grainy like the surface of a photograph.

I look at the screen. The picture swims in and out of thick pixels. First the hood of a black Mercedes appears. One fender has the Polish flag fixed to it; the other has the Georgian flag. It seems to me that the Mercedes is heading along the airport highway, toward Tbilisi. A police escort driving ahead of the car is reflected through the windshield. The cameraman shakes the objective lens. For a second, the shot shows the president of Poland, Lech Kaczyński, and a couple of sturdy bodyguards. The camera returns to the hood. Just as the Mercedes pulls level with the BP building, the foremost cars of the escort get riddled with shots simultaneously from different sides. The first car slowly peters to a stop, then bumps into the highway guardrail. The honeycombed windshield of the second car gets red-splashed with fresh blood. The third one explodes right on the spot, its passenger compartment and wheels blazing. The cameraman works miracles with his camera. The shot shakes and stops for a couple seconds. White vapor seeps out of the Mercedes' hood. The car where the cameraman is sitting suddenly pulls level. The cameraman turns the camera around sharply. From the BP side, several militants, their faces covered with black masks, run toward the car, some of them pointing their guns at the camera, others shooting up into the air. The focus is no longer any good. One of the militants walks with a slight limp, though he seems used to his artificial limb. Wrapped around his head is a green bandage with the Al Jazeera logo in white, twisted lettering. There's a black attaché case in his hand.

The militants throw the passengers out of the Mercedes. The video vanishes for a short while. The next shot shows Kaczyński on his knees in the middle of the highway, his hands clasped behind his head, two of his bodyguards beside him on their knees. The militants point guns at them. The cameraman zooms up to the limit on Kaczyński's face.

The limping militant ties the president's hands behind his back with nylon rope, and sticks an adhesive bandage over his mouth. Afterward, he opens the attaché case and gives Kaczyński a sign with a nod of his head. The latter gets up—an actor who knows his part well—and obediently sits lamb-like in the attaché case. The militant shuts it as a military 4WD off-road vehicle pulls up beside him. He hops in, putting the attaché case on the floor between his legs. The rest of the militants hit the bodyguards in the face with the barrels of their guns. They do that brutally and hard. It seems the cameraman gets hit, too. The shot focuses on the worn-out boots of one of the militants. The image fades out.

The vision vanishes. The street sweeper is still cleaning the park entrance, and the Zhiguli driver leans back in his seat the same way. My hands go numb, my ears ring.

A no. 21 bus stops before me. A ten- to twelve-year-old girl presses her nose up against the window glass, so that the glass goes steamy around her nostrils. She looks straight into my eyes through a pair of silly-looking glasses. Nobody gets off. The bus door closes with a wheeze. NEXT STOP—NATO is written in capital letters all along the side of the bus. At both ends of the message, the five-star Georgian flag and the navy blue NATO flag with four beams meet edge-to-edge. The slogan is absolutely post-hyperrealistic. *The simulation of something which has never really happened.* The bus jolts away. The girl doesn't take her eyes off me.

4. I CAN JUMP DOWN

I stand on Miho's balcony, a cigarette in one hand, a glass in the other; there's just one gulp left. Vodka martini: a popular, classic kind of drink. I look down at the street. The balcony is on the second floor; I could just jump down. The balcony door is open. Soft, minimal techno pumps from the speakers indoors—the beat bores through the music so laboriously that I can hardly keep from imagining myself in a dentist's office. Inside, Miho and Nina fuck. They're asking me to shoot them screwing with a video camera.

"Get in here," Miho calls. "Be a buddy, be a buddyroo."

"All right," I say.

I hate to be in on this stuff, it's the last thing I want. The fact is that my ex-girlfriend is screwing my friend. We broke up a week ago. It happened fast, with no showdown, no argument. You don't always need words to break up. So we didn't make a big deal out of it . . . I didn't even think it happened like that in real life, or that I would go through it. Lines I picked up from movies popped out of my mouth just like toast from a toaster. Emotionless as robots, we limited ourselves just to end-of-the-day phrases: *I'm not worthy of you . . . I'm not worthy of you either . . . I'll still love you . . . I'll still love you, too.* And now, pretending like we didn't spend the last four months together, she fucks Miho. She might have fucked him before, too. One can hardly dig the truth out of Nina.

I wonder if Miho has already discovered the ins and outs of her vagina, and whether making love to her reminds him of dancing on a volcano. Personally, I was always careful with Nina, especially in bed. Her vagina always reminded me of the Bermuda Triangle. I mean, you can't see anything on the surface, though it holds a lot of surprises. The neck of her womb is so sensitive and spongy, she can easily contract it down to the size of needle's eye, and then stretch it from California to Manhattan. Let alone her lips—she can use them as garden clippers if she needs to.

"You're not jealous, are you?" Nina asks me.

I put the glass on the handrail and turn around. She's on all fours, her tits shaking slightly. From where I stand, I can't see the cellulite starting to develop along her waistline. She looks into my face, her thick eyebrows joined Frida Kahlo-like above her nose.

Super-strong and super-naked Miho, black-tinted sunglasses on his nose, slowly screws Nina from behind to the beat of the music. Pumped and muscly, with clear-cut abdominals, a strong jaw, and a fair-haired crew cut, he looks like the universal soldier from the movie *Universal Soldier*. Ledger's Joker smiles from a poster on the wall. A crumpled paper bag marked "Scriabin's Donuts" and an open pizza box with scraps of sausage and pizza, plus the butt of a cigarette, lie on the table by the mirror. Scriabin's Donuts is a French bakery, but I have no idea what donuts or the composer Scriabin have to do with each other, or a patisserie. Maybe the baker's name is also Scriabin?

I know where the video camera is, but I still ask Miho, "Where's the video camera?"

"Over there, next to the CDs." Miho points to the shelf. "See?"

"I could jump down," I tell him.

"What's that?" Miho adjusts the glasses on his nose.

"Yeah," I say. "Coming."

I look outside again. Through the window of the house opposite, I see the legs of a man lying on a sofa and the shadow of a woman sitting at a table in front of a mirror, her long hair tied with a white ribbon. She smokes a cigarette, massaging her face with cucumber skin.

Two armored vehicles carrying Georgian flags are stationed

at the corner of the street, one of them blocking St. Petersburg Street, and the other Kamo Street. Some officers smoke, Kalashnikov guns strapped to their shoulders. Several privates drag sandbags from the street corner, leaving them in an impromptu trench so as to make space for a weapons arsenal. Is this the way the army is going to defend the city, or is this just a simulation of defense? I don't know. The garbage can under the balcony stinks bad. Bibi Sartania stands nearby, watching the soldiers messing around. In one hand he holds a beer bottle, but the other is in his pocket—I wonder if he's stroking his cellulite-ridden cock.

I haven't seen Bibi for six months. I didn't even know he was alive. He wears shabby sneakers, dirty jeans, and an oversized black T-shirt. He has a lame hat on, too, with the abbreviation NYPD on the front. He has an O-shaped tattoo around his arm, just like an arm strap. He had it inked on ten years before in Goa. He's one of those beautiful losers that swarmed Tbilisi back in the late nineties. Now they've died out like the dinosaurs. Had Bibi not gotten hung up on vint, he might even have become a founding father of Georgian ambient; he had all it took to make it happen—a cool laptop supplied with sound programs, camouflage gear with side-pockets, and military boots with fluorescent shoestrings. He was even popular, up to a certain limit; once he made the cover of *Reflection* magazine, if nothing else . . . and he played some late-night bars from time to time.

All of a sudden our last meeting comes to mind, and like a Polaroid camera my brain prints out a snapshot.

Typical Tbilisi winter, warm and with no snow as usual. However, Bibi still wears his stupid, ugly anorak with its artificial fur-lined hood. He sits alone on the terrace of McDonald's on Marjanishvili Street, drinking a vanilla milkshake through a straw. He reminds me of both the guy from the well-known video of UNKLE and some B movie crack dealer. Stinks just like a glamorous hobo, too. Sour cabbage would smell about the same way if you scented it with some exotic perfume. He hands me the vanilla shake as I approach.

"Thanks," I say, "I'll buy myself one."

"Have it," he says. "Have it."

I sip the milkshake. It tastes awful, though. The milkshake part is thirty percent, the vodka seventy. A hot, unpleasant feeling stirs in my stomach. He smiles.

"The recipe is mine."

"I never doubted that."

Soon, things start progressing in the normal way. We leave McDonald's for his one-room apartment on Klara Tsetkin Street. The kitchen looks painfully familiar: decorative wallpaper, an Orsk fridge with a broken handle (that's why a chair is always leaning against it), a greasy, ancient gas cooker, and a bright green, round ceiling lamp which hangs from a spiral-like wire, the kind old-fashioned telephones once had.

I have no idea how long we've been talking; that is, how long Bibi has been talking, talking my head off. He's surprised that Franz Ferdinand are bestsellers in Tbilisi, and says he'll form a band and call it Gavrilo Princip. We laugh our heads off like two idiots at this corny joke.

What else? An untouched hamburger wrapped in crinkly McDonald's paper with grease spots on it; an opened plastic container of peach yogurt.

I get glassy-eyed with drink, the state in which you keep on boozing but feel so juiced that 2 times 2 equals 31,972,541. What's more, you enter into any problem like a knife entering butter, and your own yeasty, dough-like body rises before your eyes. Neither sleep nor booze takes you.

We don't turn any music on. My ears still ring and sing though, just like at a disco nightclub. Shortly afterward, everything in sight goes flat like a black-and-white photograph and starts to pulse intermittently and hurriedly, like a troubled heartbeat. Only Bibi remains 3D and in color, standing out like a paint swatch against a blank wall.

Then two men come in. That's exactly like Bibi; you never know who'll come or go next. One of the two is Koka Margiani, aka Margo: next-door neighbor, thrill-seeker, photographer, and glue-sniffer. Very slow-moving. He's like an astronaut in space, his eyes not quite friendly. Looks like he was abused as a kid. He always wears a khaki bag slung over his shoulder like a field doctor, in which he keeps four tubes of Moment glue, neatly folded plastic bags, and cockroach-repellent spray for extreme cases. Once sat in a chair, he looks at me with suspicion.

One-eared Goggia follows him in. The story goes that once he got himself into a jam and some malicious people cut his ear off. The old wino, his hands trembling from too much drink, wears Dr. Marten's— the same ones that Bibi once wore—and a shabby, khaki pilot jacket with the American flag on the shoulder. Stinking, unshaven, and unwashed, he simultaneously resembles Eduard Shevardnadze and a character from a Kusturica film. Speaking of Shevardnadze, a great many people wrongly consider him an absolute good-for-nothing. But he is wonderfully recyclable. You could make a perfect S&M kit from his skin: a latex mask with a zippered mouth, a muzzle, a whip, and a set of handcuffs. His skin is tight and resilient at the same time. But speaking of presidents, I think it's about time we made more valuable things out of them. One could do without their memoirs and their philanthropy. Bibi hands Goggia a full glass. Before taking it, the latter produces a CD from the pocket of his pilot jacket and puts it on the table next to the hamburger. No words whatsoever are needed to understand that he means to say he has not come empty-handed either.

It just doesn't make sense to me. I had thought Goggia and a CD completely incompatible, like Bigfoot and a smartphone. It's got to be old rock—Yes or ELP or something of that kind. "Best of Ryoji Ikeda," say letters written in a blue marker. Well, this borders on fantasy. My brain, overtaken by drink, tries in vain to figure out what Goggia's doing with an Ikeda CD . . . and who the fuck Ikeda is, for that matter.

"There now . . . good morning, girls," says Goggia in an infernal voice, gulping down vodka and eagerly sniffing the yogurt; one pink nipple and a tattooed profile of Stalin are displayed on his hairless chest. In the next moment, his chest gets so wrinkled that the Man of Steel resembles a young Omar Sharif.

Margo seems restless. Perhaps his brain wants glue. He shuffles zombie-style into the next room, sits in an armchair, and produces a plastic bag. He carefully opens one tube of Moment, and neatly empties the contents into the plastic bag. Then he puts the bag over his head, which immediately gets steamy. Next minute, his petrified eyes appear through the plastic. His swollen face soon settles down, though. He sits in the armchair like he's in a space vehicle, and looks down at his own feet the way an astronaut surveys the earth through the viewing port. The rest of us are just around like the moons of a big planet. Even the plastic bag over his head looks like part of an astronaut's spacesuit.

Bibi passes me a glass. The kitchen starts to flicker before my eyes, just the way a cheap TV screen does. Then the kitchen wavers and lights up. Something snaps and it goes pitch dark all at once . . .

I look down at the street again. Bibi sips beer, then throws the empty bottle into the garbage can. The woman is no longer visible through the open window; all I see is the cucumber skin on the vanity table, and the feet of the man lying on the sofa. The soldiers finish setting up the trench. Just then, a provocative plaque on the front of the house opposite catches my eye:

The Department of Health advises:
Regular sex is good for your health

Good Sex, Good Family

Does the message mean that somebody's fighting against the lack of sex in Tbilisi? That seems promising. Tbilisi is indeed low on sex, and that's causing plenty of severe physical and moral perversions. Nevertheless, one single promotional effort won't take care of the problem—that is, it won't get Tbilisians fucking. However, some sex is better than no sex at all. In southern countries, revolutions should start with slum dwellers rather than white collars.

"You don't give a fuck, do you?" Miho asks me, still fucking Nina from behind.

She looks into my face again. I wonder what her orgasm is going to look like. Usually her nostrils flare first, then her knees tremble, and finally she starts to moan, her eyes rolling up.

"Okay, okay, I'm coming," I say.

I grind out the cigarette in my empty glass and enter the room. The smell of sweat, antiperspirant, sex, and pizza mix together. The Joker looks in my direction, though above my head. Minimal techno plays on the stereo, so smooth that you can't tell where one composition finishes and another starts. Miho, tied to Nina, doesn't stop; rhythmically swaying backward and forward, he adjusts his slipping-off glasses. Nina's small tits wobble from side to side.

5. THE ELECTRONIC DOG

Tina sits in the car with the door open, exposing her long legs, which hang out of the car. An open laptop lies in her lap. She's talking to Naniko through Skype. I walk up to the Peugeot, avoiding being spotted by the laptop camera. I don't feel like talking to Naniko. Tina lights a cigarette. I make an "I'm not here" gesture. The parking lot is full of SUVs the size of freight cars. Next to them, our Peugeot 207 looks even smaller than it really is.

"What did you say?" asks Naniko.

"Nothing." Tina drags on the cigarette. "What? Your voice got lost."

"No-thing." Tina blows the smoke at the camera. "Forget it."

Naniko is just like a family member. Like a TV set. Like a pet dog. Like a brownie. Though she lives in London, she's always online. Her face has not come off screen since she discovered Skype. She's an awful gossip. If you stitched her mouth up, she'd speak through her asshole.

Naniko is not quite a bad girl. If nothing else, she moved to London a year ago with her rocker-husband, who, according to her, traded heroin for methadone with the greatest of ease—truly an accomplishment worth a note in Wikipedia. Not that it'll do him any good. How can an Armenian musician from Tbilisi impress anyone in London without heroin? On the other hand, Naniko claims he's making the big time. She says he met Placebo's producer, who promised to introduce him to Brian Molko. It's something at any rate, and it seems promising—if only Naniko was trustworthy. When it comes to London, Armenians have never really had any special sway. But whatever.

Naniko would have been a lot sweeter had she not persuaded

herself that renting a studio apartment in London and getting preventive collagen injections into her lips represented the peak of success. I've got to admit it though, Naniko has made herself noticeably more sophisticated. London had its impact on her, and a very fast one for that matter. Just like in that Fatboy Slim video where prehistoric plankton evolves into Homo sapiens. You would hardly guess that she was born in Digomi. She rarely gets trashy these days. Rarely, but it's intense when she does. Sometimes Digomi radiates so intensely out of Naniko that you immediately forget about London and Placebo. She will definitely never set the Thames on fire, but she keeps true to her own ambitions. At the very least she is supposed to meet Molko himself *any day now*.

"They bombed Vake, didn't they?" Naniko is restless. That's just the way it is. All suburbanites care about is Vake.

"I told you they didn't," answers Tina. "Not yet."

"What's going on in the city? Panic?"

Amico, our trainer, comes out of the swimming pool building and skips down the walkway all dressed in white, sneakers included. His white T-shirt is so tight that you'd think it would burst open. The shoulder-to-shoulder legend across it reads "Allah Akbar." I don't get it. The world's most-wanted terrorist went out of fashion a long time ago, and not much Arabic stuff is of immediate interest either. Besides, nobody gives a damn about September 11, even if the anniversary is just a month away. Aside from that, he's all right: slickly tanned, pale-blue contact lenses, a beauty spot that he had attached to his right cheek two weeks ago. The tight T-shirt shows his prominent, pumped-up abdomen. The boxing trunks complement his dick perfectly. His body is as muscular as Schwarzenegger's. He even looks like a Terminator. Amico is always glad to see me. I feel good around him, too. All this doesn't go beyond the bounds of decency; we both know that nothing could work out between us. However, deep down I might even like him to want me. No doubt he'd gladly fuck me on the spot, no matter whether he's a cocksucker or an ass-man. However, I don't think any definition of this exists that's not made up by homophobes.

"*Buenos días*, Mr. Muscle!"

"How you doing, babe?" He gives me a kiss on the cheek, his lips making a smacking sound: *smack*!

"I'm all right. How are you?"

"Not that good." He falls silent abruptly. *Does he want me to ask what happened?*

"What happened?" (I do ask.)

"I'm being drafted into the army."

"Into the army?" I repeat stupidly. I can't imagine Amico covered in war paint like a commando, a bandage wrapped around his head, a bazooka in hand, a machinegun over his shoulder, and grenades in his pockets.

"Yeah. Got the draft notice yesterday."

Something must be wrong with his hormones, since he always uses plenty of cologne. Even the sweetest cologne can't completely kill the stink of sweat. Looking at Amico, all dressed up in white, I involuntarily recollect that white bottle of Jean-Paul Gaultier perfume, *Fleur Du Male*. A man's body and balls locked in tights like a male ballet dancer's.

"Amico!" somebody calls him from inside the building.

"Okay, got to go," he tells me. He hands me an iPod with the earphones wrapped around it. "It's Tina's, isn't it?"

This gesture's supposed to be quite heart-stirring, showing Amico to be considerate as hell. But if you got to know him well enough, you'd understand that all he meant by this was that all women are careless and forgetful, just like Tina. Sometimes Amico is simply unbearable.

"She left it?" I laugh.

"In the locker room." He raises his eyebrows and rolls his eyes.

I want to tell him that all this is starting to look like maso-
chism, bro. You played your part perfectly, so no need to overact
it. I say nothing though, only give him a wink.

He walks back to the walkway fast. His ass is perfect—tight
and well-shaped, his briefs showing from under his boxing
trunks. At the railing he suddenly turns around and looks me up
and down.

"You look good."

"Honest to God, I'm all on edge." Naniko's still restless.

"Listen," says Tina. "I'll call you later in the evening. From my
place. Okay?"

"Here they're reporting that gas masks are being handed
out in Tbilisi. The government fears a chemical attack may be
launched."

"Naniko, take care!" Tina waves her hand and closes the laptop.

I get into the car, throwing my bag on the back seat. I feel good.
Swimming is the best antidepressant. I put my head on Tina's shoulder to show her that my sympathies are with her. I want to stand by
her, want her to trust me, to need me. Women hang on to things
like this. Such trivial gestures are sometimes more important than
orgasms. A woman should be reassured that the man beside her is
not just a player, a cold-blooded fucking machine. Sometimes she
should catch your meaningful look (*you* should make her catch it,
I mean): an admiring, caring, fawning little look. I kiss her on the
shoulder, and then straighten my back in the seat. The key point
here is not to lose a sense of perspective. Tina squeezes my knee so
that I understand right away that she trusts and needs me.

How should we trust one another? I don't get it.

She turns the key. The radio goes on as she does it.

"Some time ago, Russian air forces dropped still more bombs
on the territory of Tbilisi Botanical Garden. Two hectares of
wood are on fire . . ."

I switch from the radio to the CD player. Sweet Sakamoto oozes honey-like from the speakers. You might think yourself in a candy store.

Tina puts a half-smoked cigarette to her lips. Involuntarily, I look at the nail with polish off. She sees my glance, then looks down at the nail.

"Do you want to smoke or should I throw it?" she asks.

"Give it to me." I take the cigarette.

We drive out of the parking lot. All of a sudden, Nessie, a shaggy dwarf poodle, runs out of the watchman's booth. She runs after the car, barking hard at the front wheel. I'm positive she'll go back as soon as she's run ten meters. She's programmed to do so. I've been visiting this swimming pool for a year now and know her battle style well; she runs like crazy after every set of wheels that pass within ten meters of the booth. There is something militaristic to her spirit. She is unbelievably fast at all this. Even the electrically powered dog from the miniseries *The Adventures of Elektronik* couldn't run that fast.

"Look what you left in the locker room." I show the iPod to Tina.

Just then, I notice that instead of the standard Apple earphones, which are no good, the iPod has a Bang & Olufsen pair wrapped around it.

Tina touches the earphones. "That's not my iPod."

6. BLUE VELVET

"Khinkali are cool," says Aneke.

I say nothing. She sucks the dumpling's juice with a squelching sound, then lets steam out of her mouth: "Whooo . . ." Hopefully she will fall silent now, at least for a while. I vaguely remember last night. We drank hard. My headache is splitting. I can't touch the food.

There are three of us in Blue Velvet: Gigi, Aneke, and myself. Or me and Aneke, to be precise. Gigi went to the john ten minutes ago, taking with him a bottle of Borjomi mineral water. He must be purging his stomach. I don't know whose idea it was to come here, or what all this gastronomic experimentation is about. All I know about Aneke is that she works as a reporter for some Dutch TV channel and speaks Georgian with suspicious fluency. I'm not sure if she's Gigi's girlfriend or not. You'd have to be crazy to feel horny about Aneke. But Gigi has always been stuck on mannish, thickset women, with big, uncooked-cutlet, Angelina Jolie-like lips. Aneke sort of agrees with me. She lets steam out of her mouth just like a dragon: "Whooo . . ." Her kind are called "cosmopolitan." Just one look at her is enough to get that she's full of touristic wisdom; that is, of American optimism, English vanity, German pragmatism, Russian carelessness, and Chinese obedience. And right now she's filling up on Georgian khinkali.

I have no idea what her sense of humor is like. Nor do I know how she can consciously wear a tight black T-shirt. On the shoulder of the T-shirt there's an orange mash-up of the Yohji Yamamoto logo and the sacred syllable, a sort of fashion-mantra:

Blue Velvet. That's what a high-class khinkali bar on Sharden Street just between the Pancake House and the Steak Bar gets called. Why just Blue Velvet, and not, say, *Salò, or the 120 days of Sodom*? I mean, we're talking about a khinkali bar. It's not just that Lynch's movies are considered "classy" among the Tbilisi elites, given that Pasolini's are also considered classy. But it seems that it takes more than just business acumen to name a khinkali bar Salò. You've got to be determined to do it. And Blue Velvet is just that kind of precious nonsense that Tbilisi elites can't make sense of, even though they accept it eagerly. It's symptomatic of something, in any case.

Speaking of khinkali bars—given that this one is on Sharden Street—if I owned one, I'd definitely name it Salò and hire one crazy waiter, whip in hand, to stand guard over all the customers, shouting: "*Mangia! Mangia!*" This show would be on the house, absolutely free. Or on me personally, I mean. Blue Velvet wouldn't have been too bad a name had they not made blue the dominant color of the building's interior. Inside, blue is everywhere: chairs, tables, lights, curtains . . . The brick walls feature a huge plasma screen and black-and-white stills from Lynch's movies. The plasma screen shows stills, too; views of Tbilisi pop up on the screen one after another: the Botanical Garden, Narikala Fortress, the Trinity Cathedral, the Sulphur Baths, Metekhi Fortress, Bread Square, Mtatsminda Mountain . . . a regular touristic walking tour. What the hell has Lynch got to do with all this anyway? Moreover, this visual trip is accompanied by the soundtrack to *Twin Peaks*. The speakers spill out Angelo Badalamenti's score, with Julee Cruise crooning. How many times will I wonder whether

Cruise is mimicking Elizabeth Fraser of Cocteau Twins? Or just sounds like her? Or both?

Now and then, a horrible stink comes from somewhere, so rotten that it kills even the smell of beer. The smell brings memories of my first love back to me. She was my neighbor, Matsatso. Twice my age. She had no husband. I wanted to be the one instead. To be her lover, her vagina-packer. Just to be allowed to enter her once a month, at the very least. I loved everything about her: her look, her smile, her gestures. Even her lousy name, *Matsatso*. It became my daily mantra: "Matsatso . . . Matsatso." The woman of my dreams. I loved each square millimeter of her body, thinking her unreachable, just like a Hollywood starlet. I don't have the faintest idea why, and what I was ashamed of, but I did and I was. I was embarrassed that I loved her, and that I secretly sent poems to her, other people's poems to boot. I was ashamed of my timidity. When our eyes met, she would smile meaningfully, kind of crawling inside my soul. At moments like this, I would think she knew about the trouble I was in. I would shrink away— poom-poom-poom—just like Mario turning into Luigi. I don't even remember if she was pretty or not. All I remember is that I was about to graduate high school, and the girls on my block gave lousy blow jobs or practiced ass-fucking, keeping their cherries for their future husbands. Depeche Mode was hot then, so I was supposed to be a fan of theirs, though really I was stuck on Madonna, with her muscles and conical costumes. At the same time, I was head over heels in love with Matsatso. She had a fine, somewhat thickset body, and big, natural, Monica Bellucci-type boobs. I lived on Tskneti Street those days, in block three, sixth floor. She lived on the tenth floor. Once I bumped into her in the elevator. It was summertime. She wore an above-the-knee short skirt and a tight white shirt which clearly showed the contours of her rare-meat-colored bra. It became hot in the elevator very quickly. I almost shit my pants, being so close to her. My heart beat fast, my hands sweating. The elevator moved up, slow and staggering. Time drew on too, rubber-like. How I hated and loved Matsatso at that moment! Like a movie starlet. I loved each square millimeter—her dyed hair, her lips heavily dabbed with lipstick, her eyebrows neatly plucked, and her boobs packed into the flower-pink bra as if she kept some secret there, like the X-files from the series *The X-Files*. I can't remember what she asked me. Something broke down inside me; her breath stank of rot . . .

My whole body aches. Gigi is still absent. Could he have gotten sick in the john? I don't want to take the trouble to check on him. Blue Velvet is packed. The atmosphere is saturated with a blend of expensive suits, collagen lips, and porcelain teeth. A cloud of body odor, khinkali steam, and cigarette smoke hangs just below the ceiling. The ventilation system seems to be out of order. I catch scraps of conversation here and there:

"D'you know that Berlusconi was the one who talked Putin out of bombing Tbilisi?"

"When is Sarkozy getting here?

"Berlusconi is Kaladze's buddy . . ."

"Bush returned home from the Olympic games . . ."

"America may hit Russia . . ."

". . . because of Georgia . . ."

Somebody orders: "Forty khinkalis, three kebabs, four beers—"

"Which beer?" The young waitress wants to be sure.

The Georgian elite are scattered here and there, too. There are a couple of local politicians, Telman the barber, and that random charming guy who's everywhere, I'll call him Bubba—a true Tbilisian, with his macho, homeboy vibe. Some American general is here too, with several Georgian officers. The general is a real five-star type, like a human luxury hotel. Not the officers, though. Just fake mobsters with slick hair, bandanas under their shirts and around their necks, and dark glasses on their noses. They look like drug lords and male models at the same time. Desperate housewives, explorers of Paulo Coelho's life and books, national heroes—that is, contenders in the Eurovision Song Contest—they're all here, united by khinkali, united by the Internet, united by the song "We Are the World."

Everyone looks both ordinary and extraordinary. Just like the X-Men from the movie *X-Men*. Here you can find the kind of people who think that the "airy voice" of Julee Cruise is angelic. *I want you rockin' back inside my heart* . . . The khinkali, too, looks so cute you might consider its wrapped style "haute couture." Sort of like culinary arabesques.

You hardly see so many Georgians in one place anywhere but in a khinkali bar. However, people can unite over something other than khinkali. They did this just the day before yesterday. Just for a moment, but anyway they did it. What I mean is that two days ago, students from the Academy of Art orchestrated a true perform-ance. A hundred boys and girls all in a row, synchronically and proudly, just like Riverdance dancers, drew down their pants and shit before TV cameras all along George W. Bush Street. Oh, it was more than just a spectacle. A true triumph! It stands to reason that police forces rapidly broke up the rally. Plenty of the students ended up in jail, others in the hospital. And all of them as one were dismissed from the academy the same day. Anyway, it was quite the thing to see live on CNN or BBC: a hundred craps neatly in a row all along George W. Bush Street. It's hard to keep from being proud of such simple nobility. At the moment, I'd take those craps over the world treasury. Even now I'd settle for the former. That is, they both mean one and the same shit to me. Freud was not so dog-dick stupid as to think crap a symbol of wealth.

"You for Obama or McCain?" I hear from somewhere behind my back.

The voice rings a bell. I don't want to trouble myself by turning around. Tbilisi is too small for everybody not to know one another.

"They're both the same fuck to me," answers another voice.

A young waitress passes by. She wears a horrible uniform—a white, short-sleeve shirt and blue capris. She looks like an airline attendant, lacking only a light-blue tie and a big smile. She's got a classic Georgian body: short legs, fat lips, and a flat, pear-shaped ass. Though she looks dead tired, her steps are fast and short, as if she were sliding iron-like through the air. Three empty mugs of beer with foam on the bottoms in one hand, a plate full of khinkali tops in another. She walks by so close that I distinctly make out traces of red lipstick on the tops.

My cell phone beeps on the table . . . Gigi has sent me an SMS that reads, "Abkhazia is our main trouble." I don't get what he means, but I couldn't care less. So long as he's able to send messages, the old boy is still alive. It's just like him: think great thoughts while being sick, and then the other way around—get sick thinking great thoughts. I don't want to take the trouble to reply. I put my phone on the table. Everybody and everything in Blue Velvet is blue-ridden because of the ultraviolet light. Like in a tanning bed . . . or a sci-fi thriller. A feast of the living dead, or *The Great Yokai War*. But Takashi Miike just can't compete.

Aneke can't stop; khinkali tops are heaped up on her plate. She eats relentlessly anyway. Looking stressed, she picks up another one robotically, noisily sucking in the juice. I realize too late that I am enchanted and petrified. Her mechanical moves are as exact as a mathematical formula. Those who think khinkali are just food are wrong. To a greater degree, khinkali is a phenomenon beyond mere food. Georgian DNA, Georgian spirit, Georgian insanity, Georgian folk tales—that's what it is. You can't grasp it. Rather, you should sense it. Aneke seems to be the one who senses it. She *wants* to sense it, to be part of it. Khinkali hits everywhere, viruslike. It's obvious even now that eventually a partnership will emerge victorious from the banal battle between khinkali and McDonald's. Consequently we'll get McKhinkali—

another mutant, a sort of gastronomic centaur. In the meantime, I think of the craps from yesterday, managing to watch Aneke at the same time. She sucks the juice out of another khinkali and happily gives me her European smile, a bit of parsley sticking to her front teeth.

"Are they cool?" I ask her.

"Whooo . . ." She lets steam out of her mouth.

7. VOLUME TWO/
THE INCREDIBLE HULK

Cheap paperback detective fiction, rolled-up posters of soccer players, tiny laminated icons, Hannah Montana stickers, and multi-colored pens topped with pink fluffy pompoms are neatly laid out on the right side of the newsstand, below newspapers exposed behind glass. Between the detective paperbacks, I catch a glimpse of a familiar book cover.

Even the works of Gurdjieff and Castaneda are nothing compared to certain books you occasionally hit upon in the newsstands of Tbilisi. It's really true, the former being a charlatan from Fontainebleau and the latter a mystic from California. (Neither of them, however, were French or American. They both belonged to poor southern countries.) This doesn't necessarily mean that you'll come across Derrida's *Dissemination* or Deleuze and Guattari's *Capitalism and Schizophrenia*. Pepperstein's *Mythogenic Love of Castes* is quite sufficient.

I take the earphones out of my ears, leaning toward the newsstand display. From a pocket-sized radio neatly placed on a heap of newspapers, comes the alarmed voice of a newscaster: ". . . the Vaziani Airport and the surrounding area has been bombed twice today by the Russian aircraft. Eight people are allegedly dead and twenty are injured after the air raid . . ."

"One minute please . . ."

The saleswoman looks up from her copy of *Sarke* and turns down the volume on the radio.

"Can I see that book?" I say, awkwardly pointing. "That one."

"Which?" the woman looks over her glasses, down at the books. "The one in the middle, with the decorations."

"Akunin?" She points.

"No, no. A little farther sideways."

"This one?" She puts her finger on Oksana Robski.

"Well, you're almost there," I say. "Just under it."

"This?"

"Exactly."

I take the book. It's not quite what I thought. Everything is identical, to be sure: the format, the cover, the title. But it's the second volume. The same lousy design and worthless paper—even the same distant smell of typographical ink. I'd thought volume I was a sort of acid-Bible. I had no idea that volume II even existed. It might turn out to be a big chunk of shit, though.

All of a sudden I start to remember volume I: the somnambulistic journey of a lunatic member of the Communist Party into his own hallucinosis. What I mean is that he went somewhere in the middle, where hallucination and verbal diarrhea mix, and almost at once the resulting combination started to mutate. This mutant-vision created within itself scores of overlapping waves within waves, reflecting millions of levitating, holographic images, which at the same time served as visual drugs, aural sedatives, and sexual stimulants. A house of mirrors would produce an effect that's almost the same, were it strapped to a rollercoaster.

I remember well that volume I was not for the faint-hearted. Each chapter left me smiling for a long time, just like after a good trip. By the way, books like this, the smile-hazardous ones, should have some kind of sign on their back covers somewhere near the barcode. Just to prevent certain readers from smiling eternally. The same way some DVDs have age limits on them. A sign like this would suit:

"How much?" I ask the saleswoman.

"Price is on the back side."

I turn the book over.

"No price here."

"Give it to me." She reaches for the book, looks at the cover, then pulls a notebook out of nowhere, looking inside for where she keeps some weirdly elaborate up pricing system.

"Pe . . ." she says to herself, turning over a page and dragging her index finger all the way down to some diagram. "Pe . . . here's Pepperstein. Nine laris."

Producing a twenty-lari banknote, I catch a glimpse of the latest issue of *Glamour* magazine, featuring Milla Jovovich smiling like a horny lamb. A gold-studded dress, pale makeup, and seventies-style hair à la Jane Fonda, with corrugated waves cut in the front. The photographer and makeup artist really went overboard: high cheekbones, meaty lips with claret lipstick, and a rather massive chin all shine at once. She has the glare of a randy cyborg, her eyebrows raised and her nostrils flared, as if on the verge of orgasm. Someone's flesh is reflected in her dark-greenish eyes.

"The *Glamour*, too," I say.

The woman gets flustered: "Pepperstein or the *Glamour*?"

"Both."

She hands me the book and the magazine together.

"Your change is one lari," she says. "Is it all right if I return it in coins?"

"Yes."

She hands me two fifty-tetri coins.

"Want any packaging?" she asks.

"No, thanks."

The woman turns up the volume of the radio.

I cross the street to get to the Vintage Kindzmarauli Wine House. The excited voice of the newscaster lingers in my ears for a while: ". . . Reuters reports that King Parnavaz Avenue has been occupied. The Russian tanks have entered district two. Two Turkish journalists have been reported missing . . ."

It somehow happened that the image of Milica Natasha Jovović has been following me for years. I don't chase her, she *finds* me herself. Sometimes she looks down at me from a billboard, other times from some magazine, and still other times from the TV. I've been involuntarily watching her life and work. I've seen almost all her film roles, paparazzi pictures, and photo shoots, scandalous or glamorous. I know she's a lousy star, no good at acting, fashion designing, or singing. She's a remarkable photo model, though. It's hard to tell where she looks best: on the *Ultraviolet* movie poster, in the Donna Karan commercial, or on the computer screen . . . I like her best in the photo which the Italian fashion magazine *Lei* printed on its cover in 1987. An eleven-year-old Millica looks out at you from the photo with her big, pale-blue, foxy eyes. I'd love her to give me a blow job. I just like sexy little milk-covered girls.

I approach the Vake Church. A few fighter jets, like a flock of swallows, fly overhead. Their shadows, along with a gust of wind, sweep over Chavchavadze Avenue like a gigantic fan. I lose my breath. The wind lifts the dust off the street, shaking it up into the air. An eight- or ten-year-old boy runs onto the balcony of the house across the street. He wears a black T-shirt with "The Incredible Hulk" printed on it. The boy rests his elbows on the ledge and points binoculars at the fighter jets, sunshine reflecting off the lenses. A woman in a white terrycloth bathrobe comes onto the balcony—probably she's the boy's mother. She wears a towel wrapped turban-like around her head. Talking into a cell phone, she holds a cigarette in a campy sort of way. The boy tells her something. She shades her eyes against the sun with her cigarette hand, and looks up in the direction of the fighter jets. She must be naked under that bathrobe. I love the natural smell of a freshly washed vagina. Besides the faint soap odor, they smell sort of bittersweet, the way the horizon smells during a summer sunset.

A short woman, knock-kneed and round as a barrel, comes into the churchyard, and, crossing herself, scuttles over to a dogwood-pink Toyota RAV4. She pushes the central locking button and turns off the alarm system. The car lets out a little squeal, headlights blinking for a second. The car is blessed; the windshield displays Tbilisi's all-time most popular sticker—a bronze, circular, ten-centimeter-long cross. The woman wears cream sandals, white canvas trousers, and a close-fitting shirt in lemon yellow. Either she has no breasts, or I can't tell her tits from the folds of fat on her belly. The pastel shawl thrown over her shoulders is supposed to deflect attention away from her. Only in passing do I notice that the color on her toenails matches the color of her car.

The churchyard is alive with people. I notice *chokha* and military uniforms in the crowd. I'm not sure if it's some religious holiday or a requiem service for the peace of the souls of the war dead. A couple soldiers smoke at the church gate, their rolled-up berets under their shoulder straps. Old women all in black, sitting in a row along the church fence, hold blessed candles. The women resemble zombies; they're covered in wrinkles, their faces petrified and their eyes burning.

The dogwood-pink Toyota pulls out of the line of cars parked along the sidewalk and drives off. A Hummer H3, with tinted windows and the ostentatious plate number ALIK tries to park in a vacant lot, but to no avail; it can't fit in. All of a sudden, the Hummer jumps up on the curb. The heat from the hood and the smell of engine oil hit me hard. Despite my respect for all people named Alik, it strikes me how deep-seated your inferiority complex must be to have a Hummer. Or could it be some Armenian knock-off? Georgian-Armenian, to be exact? That is, twice as fake, the imitation of an imitation, like "Georgio Armeni." I look toward ALIK. Nothing can be seen behind the heavily tinted windows. All of a sudden, the old women, encouraged, turn to ALIK, offering candles through the window. I'd hardly thought the women capable of something like this. They seem to be a seamless, well-regulated team. Just like the Sopranos in the series *The Sopranos.* The timing, speed, and precision of their movements approach the CGI effects of some big-budget movie.

"Three for a lari! Three for a lari!" they repeat, parrot-like.

A priest comes out into the churchyard, telling something to the soldiers standing at the fence. The latter listen to him carefully and obediently. The priest is just a puny little guy, the kind you could accidentally wash down the drain. He's got a red beard and bright eyes, like children have. The grandmas hesitate, looking in awe at the priest the way dogs look up at their masters. However, having made sure that the priest has given them no sign, they go over to ALIK again.

"Three for a lari!"

The priest goes back into the yard, leaving behind the mixed smell of incense and sweat, white flakes of dandruff standing out sharply on the black shoulders of his long robe. The boy is now alone on the balcony, with that ferocious-looking Incredible Hulk on his T-shirt.

8.08/08/08

♈ Aries

Your energy resources are truly limitless. The key is to mobilize them. Today, Mars leans toward the Fiery Lion. Therefore, you will be full of energy. For instance, you will absolutely be able to rape children. Don't forget, however, that they don't deserve it.

♉ Taurus

The pushier and more arrogant you are today, the easier you will obtain results, and vice versa. (You normally seek goals patiently. You prefer a game plan, a system; you're a little conservative but you still like to enjoy yourself—these are the primary qualities of a Taurus.) Now, do everything that you've always wanted to do. Let your partner know that you are capable of doing things other than baking *khachapuri*. However, hold back from having sex as much as possible, particularly if you're a young mother. Remember that in the act of childbearing, your cervix expands and loses its elasticity, which ultimately leads to the frequent escape of gas out of the vagina when under pressure. Your partner may not say anything, but he's definitely not happy about it.

♊ Gemini

Try to rest and relax. (Geminis can seldom do that.) However, today is an exceptional day. Remember that apart from global warming, the World Bank, and the war on terror, there are other things that matter. Switch yourself off from the online world. Remember your childhood: your collection of stamps, the hair you found in a cutlet bought at the school lunchroom, the videotape with music videos recorded from Super Channel, and grandpa sitting on the balcony diligently blowing soap bubbles. Have a look at some old photos. Go out into nature and breathe fresh air. Listen to light music—Puccini's operas, for example. Particularly the aria "Nessun Dorma," as performed by José Carreras. The way Carreras performs it, you might conclude he's holding a pencil in his ass. But you'll still enjoy it.

♋ Cancer

Today you might dream that you keep a Lamborghini Reventón in your garage. The 650-horsepower engine, the 6-speed transmission, and the 340 kph speed are surely limits that can't even be reached. Yet, there are cars that are even faster. A Reventón is one small miracle—not just a mere supercar, a new spin on the *deus ex machina* that many would give up both brain hemispheres for. All the more so, as a spinal cord is perfectly sufficient. Speed, extremism, and adrenaline: these three things define the modern man. And sex, lies, and videotape. As an added bonus, you might dream about the Prince of Monaco, the Sultan of Brunei, and a couple genius tycoons tied up in your horse stable. In particular, Bill Gates and Roman Abramovich. Donald Trump, too. Just in case. Dreams never kill.

♌ Leo

If two things fill your mind with new and ever-increasing wonder and awe—the starry heavens above you and yesterday's Kotex within you—don't worry. That means it's nighttime now, and it's time to change your tampon. Change it and take care of your private life. You'll be given a good opportunity to improve your career. Run the risk as you please. You'll get an opportunity to settle old issues, bringing unfinished business to an end. Indeed, all your issues begin in the past. But be careful! Don't get in too deep. It might happen that you think you have things under control, but oops! Things have *you* under control. Don't be fooled by the simplicity of this idea.

♍ Virgo

If even Valium doesn't work for you, and if you've been seeing your own reflection clearer and clearer since morning, even without a mirror, it means you're in a bad way. This is indeed elementary. Don't hesitate to turn to that special someone. He or she can't help you, but at the very least you won't be left alone face-to-face with the TV tonight. All the more so because it's been a long time since you knew whether you consume TV or it consumes you. Besides, you can't grasp which is more real: your life or the programs on the Discovery Channel.

♎ Libra

Don't get defensive over nothing. Nobody's accusing you of anything, anyway. But you shouldn't let your hair down. Deep down you do know that you're at fault. If the human mind were capable of restarting itself, every decent person would use this option now and again. However, the human mind can't do that much. Therefore, don't begin anything new today. Your efforts might irritate others. Don't forget: 1) what starts well ends badly 2) what starts badly ends terribly 3) what starts terribly never ends.

♏ Scorpio

Today you will receive a rare opportunity to return to your past and take care of unfinished business. Remember, though: sometimes questions are better than answers. Try to let things slide. Stop trying to control everybody and everything. Life will go on without your intervention. Though the start of the day may seem a little boring to you, you might cheer up by the end, once you realize that life is much easier than it looks.

♐ Sagittarius

How long have you been unable to get it up for your wife? Do you think that you need three things to get an erection—money, adrenaline, and energy? If you have none of these three things, try Viagra or pretend to be asleep. By the way, we have nothing against your formula, it looks pretty attractive:

As a matter of fact, all doors are open to you. You aren't welcome everywhere, though. Besides, your luck is testing you today. If the day passes peacefully, there's a chance you might get your short bio placed post-mortem in a Georgian wall calendar somewhere between Tea Plucker's Day and an anecdote. There's always the chance.

♑ Capricorn

Sometimes you feel that you are on the verge of some great discovery. But it's just a feeling. The greatest thing you could discover from now on is that plenty of strangers would love to strangle you, to say nothing of your personal acquaintances. Just for the hell of it. Therefore, before it happens, keep mixing with fashionable people. Today you will highly enjoy their glamorous whims, fleeting depressions, and VIP-smiles, just because nobody gives a damn about you there. You will remain completely unnoticed. But dress *correctly*. Neither copy nor ignore their style. Don't forget that the ideal suit is a kind of camouflage, the cap of invisibility which allows you to stay unseen.

♒ Aquarius

Do you feel disadvantaged? Is it difficult to make important decisions? Then repeat three times: "Here I stand and I can change." Then straighten up, stretch your arms along your shoulders, take a deep breath, and hold it. Count to fifteen in your head. Then lower your arms fast while releasing your breath, and imagine that your breath is removing your negative feelings. If the stress is still not relieved, don't hang your head lower than you usually do. Take a break. Actually, your life *is* one long break. Just try to keep smiling. It won't add anything to your charm, but your partner will like it.

♓ Pisces

Watch for a young Armenian woman. She's got short, highlighted hair, a balcony suntan, and thin, pillar-like legs. She's tiny; she'll be hiding behind a helium balloon. Her shoulders slope downward Λ-like, and her arms are soft and fluffy, like a princess's. Her favorite dish is *dolma*, her favorite band System of a Down. She'll wear a pale-blue dress and white cork wedges; an oval-shaped artificial leather bag will be over her shoulder. Her eyes may scare you, but don't give up. This woman is your destiny.

9. WAITING FOR VINT/ DIET OF HEROES

Several parked cars in the yard. A tire-less orange Moskvich, warm from the sun, is propped up on bricks. A woman on one of the balconies above beats dust out of a rug with a stick. Some children play soccer on a newly refurbished playground. The breeze brings black smoke from somewhere. A TV is heard through an open window: ". . . we remind you that the area surrounding State University, Varazi Alley across from the Central Zoo, and Kostava Street by the Amirani movie theater are mined . . ." SHAKO sits on the curb next to the Moskvich, staring at some point in space. He mechanically keeps opening and closing a push-button pocket knife. Suddenly he stops, looks around, and starts scratching something on the Moskvich door. BIBI comes out of one of the doors of the building, scratches the back of his head, and comes closer to SHAKO.

BIBI: What're you doing?

SHAKO: Waiting.

BIBI: Who for?

SHAKO: Nugo.

BIBI: He pushing vint?

SHAKO: (*Continues scratching the door, keeping his head down.*) What else would Nugo do?

BIBI: Eh . . . (*Pause.*) I want some too.

SHAKO: You've got money on you?

BIBI: Five laris.

SHAKO: (*Ironically or sadly.*) Who'd sell it for five? Ten.

BIBI: (*Surprised.*) Ten? (*Pause.*) It cost five yesterday, didn't it?

SHAKO: It's gone up, man.

BIBI: That fast? Just in one day?

SHAKO: He even pushes for twenty. It's financial crunch time, man, c-r-u-n-c-h . . .

SHAKO stops scratching the car, puts the open knife on the ground, pulls the sneaker off his right foot, looks it over carefully, pulls out the inner sole, and pokes about inside for something. Then he turns the sneaker upside down and beats it against the palm of his hand, trying to see if anything will fall out. He finds nothing, so puts his hand back inside the sneaker.

SHAKO: Where the hell's it gone . . . (*Reflectively.*) I put it here for sure.

BIBI: What're you looking for?

SHAKO: Had got some dope. (*Pause.*) Thought we might get hung up for a bit.

BIBI: How 'bout Codelac?

SHAKO: Psh!

BIBI: What you mean psh?

SHAKO: Vint is better.

BIBI: You know what I thought yesterday? (*Pause.*) That we're the vint generation.

SHAKO: So what?

BIBI: What's the English for vint generation?

SHAKO: The Vint Age.

BIBI: So in a way we're "vintage" guys.

SHAKO: You're a jerk.

Still sitting on the curb, he pulls the sneaker back on his foot, pick up the knife, and continues to scratch with it. BIBI looks around, sits down on the curb too, lights a cigarette, and drags hard.

BIBI: When Nugo said he'd come?

SHAKO: At one.

BIBI: (*Pulls a cell phone out of his pants pocket, glances at the screen.*) It's already one-thirty. (*Pause.*) You sure he'll come?

SHAKO: (*Shrugging his shoulders.*) Who the hell knows? (*Pause.*) We've got no other choice, anyway.

BIBI: If he fucks us up like yesterday?

SHAKO: He said he wouldn't.

BIBI: But he did yesterday, right? And the day before, too.

SHAKO: (*Sounding irritated.*) Oh, god, cut it out, will ya?

BIBI: You sure he won't do it today too?

SHAKO: He said he'd come at one.

BIBI: It's already one thirty.

SHAKO: So he's gonna get here soon.

BIBI: He should've already got here by now.

SHAKO keeps on scratching. A herd of bicyclists rides along the highway in the distance. They look tired, bending forward in their seats and pushing the pedals heavily. Due to their egg-shaped helmets, reflective glasses, and aerodynamic suits—which stick to their bodies—they look like the children of Robocop. A gray Ford Sierra drives behind them.

BIBI: How 'bout Lyrica? Two for each of us. Three hundred milligrams.

SHAKO: So you want us to get fucked up in the head, like crazy poets?

BIBI: The names are cool. I mean Prozac antidepressant and Lyrica painkiller.

SHAKO: (*Keeping his head down.*) Literature, man.

The squeal of a cell phone is heard. BIBI takes the phone out of his pocket, reads a message, and then types a reply.

BIBI: (*Putting the cell phone back in his pocket.*) How 'bout some beer?

SHAKO: Beer in this heat? Psh!

BIBI: Well, if he wanted to come, he'd have already got here.

SHAKO: Jesus, here we go again.

BIBI: If he fucks us up again? (*Pause.*) It's almost two. Come on, give him a buzz.

SHAKO takes his mobile out of his pocket, dials a phone number, and listens for a long time. The scene repeats. Then he returns the phone to his pocket.

BIBI: His phone off?

SHAKO: He hung up on me.

BIBI: What's that supposed to mean?

SHAKO: It means he'll get here any minute.

BIBI: If he fucks up?

SHAKO: No way.

BIBI: Jeez, I can't wait any longer.

SHAKO: Said he'd get here by one for sure.

BIBI: If he doesn't?

SHAKO: (*Happily.*) Here comes Nugo!

A short, skinny guy comes into the yard with quick steps. Stoop-shouldered, he has a few days' stubble on his face; he wears a pair of black jeans, black sneakers, and a black T-shirt. SHAKO and BIBI stand up. SHAKO no longer plays with his knife. The stranger walks to the Moskvich, turns to the block of apartments, and puts his hands up around his mouth, palm to palm, imitating a sort of voice trumpet. SHAKO and BIBI sit down again on the curb. BIBI makes his phone screen light up.

THE STRANGER: (*Shouting.*) Tina! (*Pause.*) Tina!

An elderly woman comes out on one of the balconies; she wears a striped robe. She smiles at the stranger, motioning for him to come up. The stranger enters the building.

SHAKO: He looked like Nugo from afar.

BIBI: Yeah, he did.

SHAKO: (*Looking at the stranger's back.*) He sure looks like Nugo. You know, I heard Tina was one hot chick back in the day.

BIBI: I just wonder how guys are gonna get stoned in the distant future.

SHAKO: You mean after a hundred or two hundred years from now?

BIBI: No, I mean in the far distant future. When they'll ask questions like whether the egg first came from egg powder, or whether egg powder first came from the egg, and nobody will have the answer.

SHAKO: Oh, don't fuck with me now, will ya?

SHAKO stops scratching the car door; he cleans the point of the knife with his thumb and index finger. A peculiar version of a well-known logo is now scratched into the Moskvich door:

BIBI: Wow, you're being philosophical. (*Looks at the scratched logo.*) What you mean by "Everlost"?

SHAKO: Oh God, don't fuck with me about what I mean and all. Just for the hell of it, okay?

BIBI: Okay, okay, just take it easy! I don't give a damn about it.

SHAKO: Let it go.

BIBI: (*Looks down on the cell phone screen.*) Let's get the hell out of here, why don't we? SHAKO: No way.

BIBI: What you mean no way?

SHAKO: We're waiting for Nugo.

BIBI: He's not gonna come.

SHAKO: Wait a minute, are you just pretending to be crack-brained, or you're really sick in this heat?

BIBI: Okay, go easy. (*Pause.*) You know that Amico got drafted?

SHAKO: Gay Amico? Into the army?

A police car drives into the yard, its blue and red lights blinking. SHAKO hides the knife in his hands. The car almost stops; the cops seem to be looking intently at SHAKO and BIBI. A walkie-talkie is heard from the car: ". . . people who have lost their homes will be provided with food products and articles of daily necessity. The Twenty-First Century Georgia Association has delivered clothes and soft toys to bombing victims... *The police car makes a U-turn and slowly drives out of the yard.* SHAKO *keeps on opening and folding the knife reflexively.*

BIBI: I can't stand this waiting diet.

SHAKO: You're always saying that.

BIBI: Let's go, why don't we?

SHAKO: Let's go.

They do not move.

Curtain.

10. JAPANESE STUFF

I sit alone in the taxi with all the windows open, the air conditioning off. The driver is outside, waiting as a police officer fills out a traffic ticket. It must be for driving through a red light. It's unbearably hot. The taxi driver tries hard to convince the cop that he drove through the yellow light, but to no avail. I can't hear their argument as I'm listening to my iPod, Madonna squealing: *Give it to me, yeah / No one is gonna stop me now . . .*

It's a nice iPod, 160 GB, with Bang & Olufsen earphones. You don't find earphones like these too often in Tbilisi, so I'd better not bring them to the swimming pool yet. I just wonder who the owner is. I'd gladly look into his mind. He seems to have downloaded everything from opera to ambient. It just fell into my lap. It better have. Although, I really should return it just in case Amico finds out about it. I mean, it's going to get talked about quite a lot. But then again, who's going to hit the ceiling over an iPod? Particularly one left at the Vake swimming pool? Everybody's too relaxed there to do that. And Amico's been busy with this army stuff . . . never mind that he's sure that he gave me back Tina's iPod, the one she had left in the locker room. So hopefully it's mine now.

By the way, an iPod can tell a lot about its owner. *Show me your iPod and I'll tell you who you are.*

The police officer, bent over the hood of the taxi, keeps on filling out the traffic ticket, showing he doesn't care what the driver tries to say to him. An explosion goes off somewhere very close. The taxi shakes slightly. Nearby car alarms go off. A small, frightened black dog runs across the street, its big red tits shaking. A tree-shaped air freshener hangs on the air conditioner regulator in the taxi. If you added a little honey to shoe polish, it would smell just about the same choking way. I open the glove compartment. Inside I see a black baseball cap with a splashy embroidered logo that has nothing whatsoever to do with baseball:

my magic mushrooms

I observe the cab driver in spite of myself through the car window; he's a big guy with hairy arms. The cap could hardly be his; probably somebody left it in the car. I catch sight of the cover of the new issue of *Auto Moto* magazine, where, unexpectedly, my dream looks right into my eyes: a black Hayabusa, absolutely mental stuff—the transport of philosophers (transport as in transcendental sport). The magazine is repulsively filthy. I close the glove compartment.

I connect to the Internet through my cell phone. First off, I start browsing pictures of some chick named Sheila. There's never anything interesting under *Facials*, *Real Virgins*, *Anal*, *Big Tits*, or *MILF*. What I always browse is just *Teen Girls*. The girls who are taking their first steps into the porno industry are always a lot more exciting than experienced stars. You might also find good stuff in *Amateurs* or *Hentai*. Sometimes in *Asians* as well. The fact is that Laotian and Vietnamese girls tend to get up to exotic stuff now and then that no pro will go near. This chick Sheila looks pretty nice and compact; she's got a high forehead, large eyes, big tits, and a firm belly. As usual, the first couple of stills are pretty unimpressive, what with the plot being pretty rudimentary. She wears a short black skirt, knee-high socks, and patent leather shoes. A black tie stands out against her white shirt. Sheila is in an empty lecture hall, her nose in some anatomy book. On the table in the center of the lecture hall, a corpse can be seen from under a white sheet. From time to time, Sheila takes down some notes in her notebook. She puts her hand on her knee, slides it up slowly, puts it inside her underwear, and toys with her clit. Little by little, Sheila gets so hot that she forgets about her book entirely. First she takes off her tie, then she unbuttons her shirt; next, her bra and short skirt come off. In no time at all, she's only wearing her long socks and shoes. In the ninth picture, Sheila is walking up to the table, taking the sheet off the corpse. On the table lies the bluish corpse of a handsome young man. Sheila looks down at the corpse, stroking her nipple with one hand and toying with her clit with the other. She's a tiny girl, her pubic hair still unshaven; the fluffy bush is untouched. In the next picture Sheila is already astride the table, licking the corpse's toes one by one. Slowly, she crawls up. As it turns out, even a corpse gets it up for Sheila. Her searching tongue liberates the corpse's sexual energy. She wastes no time diligently sucking the stone-hard cock of the corpse. According to expectations, the cock is big, thick, and veined Rocco Siffredi-style. Now Sheila sits on this blue cock with her tight pussy . . . I just wonder what the end of this banal story will be. But all of a sudden, the page freezes. I can't browse the site either forward or back; all I can see on the screen is the repellent message *this page can't be displayed*.

I glance at the billboard standing right in front of the Turtle Lake cable-car station in Vake. The army recruiter calls to me: CHOOSE YOUR RESERVE FORCE! The composition's simple, just like Benetton's billboard ads; the logo follows a green line that goes into the lower right-hand corner of the image. One eighth of the billboard is shadowed by the former GeoStateConst building.

The cable-cars don't work. The cars hang motionless on the cables somewhere in midair. I feel a hard-on. The recruiter has a Viagra-like impact on me; he pumps me up with his militaristic spirit. And this is absolutely right; I've never believed in that pacifist bullshit. My stomach gets harder, as if my insides are irritated. The heat gets to me so much that my cock is about to shoot cum like a mine thrower. I feel my prostate juice leak through its heated tube. I could not feel worse if I put my own dick into a mincing machine and rolled the handle myself.

It wasn't even this hot in Telavi last year. But the nightmare was almost the same; I guess it's a nightmare having a wife like Tina and not being able to fuck her; your cock being sickly red hot and your prostate juice oozing almost constantly. That was the shitty way I felt last year. I mean, I had to live without Tina for almost half of July and the whole of August, forty-five days of hell. In the hardest moments, I even imagined my penis had come off and was crawling toward the next pussy, snail-like antennas on its head. It seems like a short time now, but back then each second lasted a lifetime. I, for one, could have put up with those rural living conditions and only sleeping five hours a day had I kept Tina with me and had sex with her at night. It didn't work out that way though. Tina was forced to stay in Tbilisi to take care of her business.

Of course, I could have jerked off, despite unfavorable conditions—the point being that I shared a room with the film's director. Of course, I could have *gotten my cum out* had I wanted it that much, either in the shower or in the john. I did it twice. However, it turned out so disappointing that I didn't even try it a third time. The third time is *not* lucky. Masturbation is not my strong suit. In any case, each morning I sent Tina different pictures of my erect dick through my phone, but this didn't solve the issue. Eventually, Tina started sending pictures of her cunt in return, and that got my mind totally fucked up. Those times she epilated her pubic hair so that her bush was left cropped like an "I." I still keep in my phone a text of her swollen clit and vulval lips. Ultimately, I got so irritable that I was on the verge of blowing up. Just like a suicide bomber. If my cock were flexible enough, I would have stuck it up my own ass. I sure would've.

Just then I realized how hazardously explosive a sexually un-satisfied man is. You could expect anything from him.

On the other hand, you should expect no less from a sexually satisfied man.

Black smoke and a burning smell are coming from somewhere. I take out the earphones and give Tina a buzz to tell her I'll be a little late, but that I'm in such a state I'm about to cum through my ears, and that I can't imagine Amico in the battlefield, holding a machine gun in his hands. The call is going through when, at the last second, an operator tells me in an impersonal voice, "The number you have dialed is not registered."

My sweat-soaked T-shirt sticks to my body. Several ambu-lances, their loud sirens squealing, race down the highway. Near-by, a tow truck tows an Opel. The last to pass is a battered, cream-colored Niva that slowly growls along the road, its exhaust pipe blowing black smoke, enlarging the ozone hole. A Georgian five-cross flag flutters on a small pole jutting out the Niva window. I hear a song, too: *Hello, my Abkhazia! My blue mountains* . . . I quickly put my earphones back in, and though it's Madonna who sings into my ears, still my mind automatically finishes the Ab-khazia song: . . . *white health sanatoria.* The small black dog with big red tits sits under the garbage can fixed to a light post. She breathes heavily, her tongue hanging out, her eyes closing from the heat. *Give it to me, yeah / No one is gonna stop me now* . . .

Next to the cableway station, where the GeoStateConst build-ing used to be, there stands a giant, reinforced-concrete edifice with plate glass windows. However, the former building hasn't gone anywhere at all. The whole trick is that it's still there, in its old place—*inside the new one.* They've just put a glass front, condom-like, over the old one. This is one of Tbilisi's biggest secrets—behind many ultramodern plate glass facades, you'll find an Italian yard with laundry hanging from ropes stretched between balconies, and neighbors playing backgammon under the shadow of grape vines. The shining, perfectly smooth surface of the building seems to be asking for damage. But Tbilisi is too small for that kind of thing.

So small that not even terrorists managed to get a toehold here—nor cocaine dealers, the paparazzi, Jehovah's witnesses, or colored students in white sneakers. Turkish migrant workers (capable of adapting, like rats, to any way of living) don't count here. So nobody whose existence is essential to any capital city—mind you, in the twenty-first century—could put down roots here. The time will come when Tbilisi will probably join the ranks of cities that have iTunes. However, not even falafel has been introduced here so far, let alone a tiny sex shop someone could have opened far from downtown, in the middle of nowhere. The bite of Orthodox fundamentalism turned out to match its bark. Maybe all the average Georgian is capable of is fucking for the sake of population expansion, and just so long as it's not on a religious holiday. The only home-grown terrorist we ever had was Vladimir Arutyunian, an honest Armenian, perfect for any collection—think *Armeni Collezioni*—who tossed a grenade at George W. Bush during the latter's visit to Tbilisi. But he was secretly arrested and isolated. *No one can be a hero in a fake city.* By the way, the matter was hushed up so promptly and ruthlessly by the Georgian and American intelligence services that it became obvious right away that Vladimir was an individual actor; that is, a loose cannon, rather than a pre-packaged but disposable celebrity, created and managed by the secret services—think *Armeni Exchange.*

Presumably, toying with brand names reveals the root of the matter more fundamentally than any cultural discourse or dialectics. In the environment of a market economy, there's no difference whatsoever between a loose cannon and a disposable celebrity. And if there is one, it seems at first glance as negligible as the one between Armani Collezioni and Armani Exchange.

On the other hand, the difference between these brands is as basic as that between a normal virus and an abnormal one; it's the difference between amphetamine and methamphetamine, between planets moving along the same orbit. If nothing else, the prices are different; you don't have to be a fashion expert to know that Armani Collezioni products are a lot more expensive than those of Armani Exchange. This implies, by itself, degrees of intellectual, social, and moral difference.

The Wikipedia article about Vladimir Arutyunian is short and dry. And yet, Muntadhar al-Zaidi's well-publicized, smelly performance comes nowhere near Vladimir's (he who almost blew up the US president with a homemade grenade). This begs at once a sense of pride and regret from all mankind. I mean, it seems barely possible to perpetuate an act of terrorism against an individual who, apart from his personal security service, is protected by two hundred and fifty agents of the secret service, fifteen policemen, and four helicopters. Of course it was some left-field Caucasian affair that has nothing to do with global conspiracies. It's obvious that every nation needs an "enemy image" to consolidate against. It's clear, however, that the figure of Arutyunian can't stand in for the Georgian. Moreover, terrorist acts and, more crucially, the mimicry of these acts serve primarily to decrease a nation's self-esteem. Georgian self-esteem can't fall any lower, though. At least, it's harder than it seems on the surface. Therefore, the former GeoStateConst will be safe from danger for a long time coming.

All of a sudden, a bird darts downward from the roof of the Plexiglas building, its reflection sweeping along the glass windows. The birds lands on the shadowy edge of the billboard. The army recruiter smiles down at me.

The driver gets back into the taxi, the breeze from his movement waking up the stale, constricting odor of the car's interior. Pissed off, the driver throws his driver's license and the traffic ticket into the glove compartment (the black Hayabusa—that obscure object of desire—throws a second-long glance at me before the driver shuts it away), puts on his sunglasses, and turns the key.

The officer raises his hand; a white Mercedes pulls up before us, an "I'm Georgia" sticker on the windshield. This has lately become the most popular sticker in Tbilisi. A middle-aged woman steps out of the car. Is she really Georgia? Tanning-bed skin, and elegantly dressed in light cream from head to toe. Only her shoes bear a slight sapphire touch. They're almost the same color as a good lotion faintly tinted with mother-of-pearl, shut up inside a half opaque, half transparent tube. Her face is hidden under heavy makeup. Even wet plaster used to make a cast of a dead body is not so heavy. Despite her age, she still looks brisk and sexy. However, her vaginal lips must be less sensitive and roughened up now, looking like the droopy ears of an elephant. She has good poise, a well-groomed body, and strong arms. When she was younger, she used to play tennis or swim. Maybe she still does. Powerful thighs are visible through a knee-length dress. Messy, fair hair cut short shines softly.

The driver tells me something. I take off my earphones.

"What's that?" I ask.

"She's an awesome fuck." He points his head toward the woman, turning the wheel. He looks at her over his sunglasses.

He's a big guy, with the high-pitched, nagging voice of Celine Dion—that is, of a constipated grandma and a virginal teenage girl all at once.

I wish I could tell him something unbearably smart, something profound, Wittgenstein-style, but for that you have to be special, and I'm just a Georgian, a son of the Caucasus Mountains, which, in itself, equals a totally *different* mentality, sort of anti-Wittgensteinian. Therefore, not to ignore him completely, I say what comes to my mind first.

"Oh, for sure she is!"

I put the earphones back in. *Get stupid, get stupid, get stupid, don't stop it* . . . Again, Madonna squeals in my ears.

I smell the strong perfume of the woman through the window as we drive by her. So strong that it kills even the all-encompassing stink of the car's interior. It's got to be Japanese stuff: first comes the aromatic scent of bamboo and Chinese tea mixed with the soft odor of raw cucumber, then the scent of gardenias follow.

11.GEORGIA

robozapienz says:
　　sugar you there?
nylon_eyes says:
　　yeah
robozapienz says:
　　what you doin? still in potsdam?
nylon_eyes says:
　　no. my weekend is over ((
nylon_eyes says:
　　i'm going to berlin
nylon_eyes says:
　　still on train
robozapienz says:
　　that's why you don't have ur skype cam on?
nylon_eyes says:
　　))
robozapienz says:
　　why the hell did u go to potsdam, business?
nylon_eyes says:
　　no sugar. friends invited me to a party
robozapienz says:
　　nice))
robozapienz says:
　　and how was it?
nylon_eyes says:
　　as expected
nylon_eyes says:
　　all strictly buddhist-like: earth, wind & fire

robozapienz says:
  ha ha
nylon_eyes says:
  potsdam chainsaw massacre
nylon_eyes says:
  shit! it's raining in berlin ((
robozapienz says:
  and it's +46 in tbilisi
robozapienz says:
  I may melt like meltman
robozapienz says:
  nickelodeon tv has a series called 'action league now!' there is
  a character named 'meltman'
nylon_eyes says:
  ha ha
robozapienz says:
  ha ha
nylon_eyes says:
  how's it going? finished the book?
robozapienz says:
  almost. just some finishing touches to add
nylon_eyes says:
  soon as you're done, mail it to me
robozapienz says:
  sure thing
nylon_eyes says:
  really wanna know what's come of it
robozapienz says:
  ))
nylon_eyes says:
  you included that short story?
robozapienz says:
  which one?

nylon_eyes says:

the one you sent me that time where a guy smells analgin imagining he smells cocaine

robozapienz says:

ha ha

robozapienz says:

no it's totally different stuff

nylon_eyes says:

it's a pity

nylon_eyes says:

you're not gonna publish it?

robozapienz says:

what r you talking about?

nylon_eyes says:

what you mean?

robozapienz says:

ha ha

robozapienz says:

so long as in tbilisi one neighbor gives the other potatoes to cook borscht, nobody will publish my book

robozapienz says:

how's it going with you?

nylon_eyes says:

late september i might take part in an exhibition in amsterdam

robozapienz says:

anything interesting?

nylon_eyes says:

seems so. at least i'm 100% sure a couple interesting guys are going to exhibit

robozapienz says:

what about you? you're gonna do an installation again?

nylon_eyes says:

yeah, i've got an idea by the way. you know tetra pak cartons, right? they're for pasteurized milk and fruit juice. so i want to make this carton all black, it's gonna have just the apple logo on it in white, with the inscription "apple juice" under

robozapienz says:

ha ha cool! inscription's gonna be white too right?

nylon_eyes says:

exactly. so you like the idea?

robozapienz says:

absolutely! i figure the pack's gonna look minimalist right? like a mac laptop

nylon_eyes says:

sure

robozapienz says:

ha ha apple juice in a carton looking like a laptop is awesome

nylon_eyes says:

thnx. listen, you've seen "tokyo!"?

robozapienz says:

what the hell's "tokyo!"

nylon_eyes says:

new movie, saw yesterday, three short stories. directors: michel gondry, leos carax, and some south korean guy

robozapienz says:

sorry but i hate gondry

nylon_eyes says:

relax. i can't stand gondry either. as ever, he tries hard to look sweet and lovely but it turns out to be some bullshit story: a girl turning into a chair. korean is okay, but nothing special. but the carax movie is very cool. you have to watch it. called "merde." means shit in french. anybody comes over from tbilisi, i'll pass it on for you

robozapienz says:

thnx. gonna be cool

robozapienz says:
   http://www.youtube.com/watch?v=CD6VgRUE1y0
nylon_eyes says:
   what's this?)) you depressed?
nylon_eyes says:
   what does the music mean
robozapienz says:
   music's just the regular shit. you should turn off the sound
   only the video's awesome
robozapienz says:
   reminds me of kafka in a way
nylon_eyes says:
   kafka in what way?
robozapienz says:
   watch and you'll get it))
nylon_eyes says:
   ok
nylon_eyes says:
   will watch it later
nylon_eyes says:
   and how r u?
nylon_eyes says:
   you didn't leave tbilisi for the country?
robozapienz says:
   no and i got screwed up too. mickey mouse in da house
robozapienz says:
   well tbilisi's too quiet a city. too often. you get sick here
robozapienz says:
   i have no contact with anybody. communication with people is
   not exactly my strong suit. i'm better at observing. i deal with
   society in my own way. seems like i was a security camera in
   a former life

robozapienz says:

you know what i feel like doing sometimes? especially at night i start to want to load a machine gun tony montana-style and yell "say hello to my little friend!" and shoot everybody around

nylon_eyes says:

ha ha

nylon_eyes says:

hannah montana's tony montana's daughter

nylon_eyes says:

??

nylon_eyes says:

where r you?

robozapienz says:

i'm here sugar phone rang sorry

robozapienz says:

miss you sugar

nylon_eyes says:

you too))

nylon_eyes says:

you know who turned up at a party in potsdam?

robozapienz says:

who?

nylon_eyes says:

remember natsarkekia from sanzona?

robozapienz says:

designer natsarkekia nastia's boyfriend?

nylon_eyes says:

yeah

robozapienz says:

pizdishen zeitung!

robozapienz says:

that old bear still alive

nylon_eyes says:

he looked so cool i thought i was tripping

nylon_eyes says:

had some tight lilac colored shirt on. greased hair and all. you should've seen him dancing!

nylon_eyes says:

jesus quintana 100%. wondered why they didn't put on hotel california

robozapienz says:

performed by gipsy kings?

robozapienz says:

ha ha ha

robozapienz says:

was he alone or with somebody?

nylon_eyes says:

he turned up with some queer metrosexuals

nylon_eyes says:

we even took pictures together with my cyber-shot. i kept them

robozapienz says:

send them to me

nylon_eyes says:

will send later have no usb cord now

robozapienz says:

ok

nylon_eyes says:

listen what's going on in tbilisi?

robozapienz says:

new khinkali bar blue velvet opened on sharden and new french bakery scriabin's donuts on barnov

nylon_eyes says:

ha ha

nylon_eyes says:

i knew about blue velvet, gigi told me. first time hearing about

scriabin's donuts tho. ha ha what have scriabin or donuts got
to do with anything? particularly a french bakery?

robozapienz says:

who the fuck knows))

nylon_eyes says:

ah i can't stand tbilisi-type conceptualism

nylon_eyes says:

what else is up?

robozapienz says:

nothing special. kaczynski was released a short time ago

nylon_eyes says:

who is kaczynski?

robozapienz says:

president of poland

robozapienz says:

this morning the presidents of france, poland, the ukraine, es-
tonia, and lithuania came to georgia to sort of support us

robozapienz says:

and chechens kidnapped the president of poland from the airport highway

nylon_eyes says:

holy shit!

nylon_eyes says:

what have chechens got to do with this?

robozapienz says:

it's not all that simple. i mean it looks like the russians are
behind the chechens. matter of fact, kaczynski and saakashvili
are buddies and make up this stuff together to show the world
that the russians are fuckers

nylon_eyes says:

shit!

robozapienz says:

so a couple hours later georgian special forces conducted a

raid and freed kaczynski. people have been hanging around the parliament building all day long. kind of a horrible sight—everybody's wearing gas masks. rumors spread that they may launch chemical attacks on tbilisi. the presidents are all standing by: nicolas sarkozy, toomas ilves, valdas adamkus, and yushchenko. then bang, saakashvili takes the floor and says look what great special forces georgia has and all. then he opens his case and kaczynski jumps out with his hands tied behind his back and a band-aid on his mouth

nylon_eyes says:

jumped right out of the case?

robozapienz says:

yeah, kaczynski is short

nylon_eyes says:

not bad!

robozapienz says:

not bad at all

nylon_eyes says:

holy shit!

robozapienz says:

have been listening to charkviani's "sakartvelo" since morning, patriotic sort of stuff

nylon_eyes says:

coool

robozapienz says:

just recollecting old times, feeling sort of romantic sugar

nylon_eyes says:

ok go ahead put on sakartvelo

robozapienz says:

it's on youtube

nylon_eyes says:

thnx old charkviani is awesome respect

robozapienz says:

just thinking of the old album swan song and how none of the other georgian stuff can beat it

nylon_eyes says:

no argument

robozapienz says:

charkviani made good stuff after that too

nylon_eyes says:

yeah but i hate his pretty girlfriend

robozapienz says:

ah man i can't stand that dame

nylon_eyes says:

same with me

robozapienz says:

??

robozapienz says:

sugar you gone?

nylon_eyes says:

no. was searching youtube for sakartvelo

robozapienz says:

))

nylon_eyes says:

people in here are going fuckin nuts!! you should see their stupid faces

robozapienz says:

??

nylon_eyes says:

i got sakartvelo at max volume

nylon_eyes says:

i don't give a shit!! the whole train's gonna hear it: SA-KAR TVE-LO! SA-KAR-TVE-LO!

robozapienz says:

ur so sweet

nylon_eyes says:
  ok sugar i'm getting off
robozapienz says:
  ok
robozapienz says:
  get in touch in the evening
nylon_eyes says:
  kiss
robozapienz says:
  bye))
nylon_eyes says:
  shit it's raining hard outside
nylon_eyes says:
  got no umbrella
robozapienz says:
  ((

12. ADIBAS

Naked mannequins pose behind the window of a Lacoste shop. Inside, all the shelves are empty. Workers drag large, heavy containers outside. A pull-down ladder leans against the façade of the house; somebody's taking down the trademark crocodile logo. Are they closing down? Small wonder. It was obvious all along that Lacoste couldn't meet Tbilisian standards.

Naturally, everyone who likes to dress well goes to the Didube secondhand shops, not the designer stores in Vere or Vake, simply because you can buy things in the former that are not available in the latter. And even if they are, they're so costly even when discounted that only foreigners can afford them. Meanwhile, exactly the same things are almost free on Tsereteli Avenue.

If you want, say, a Louis Vuitton briefcase with gilded corners for fifteen laris, or black suede Manolo Blahnik shoes for twenty-five (twenty if you bargain the price down), or leather loafers by A. Testoni for ten—all you have to do is roll up your sleeves, gird yourself with an archaeologist's patience, and laboriously go through the bundles. But look what you could end up with in return: a Vivienne Westwood coat, a John Varvatos blazer, Salvatore Ferragamo cufflinks, a Bottega Veneta purse, a Peachoo+Krejberg belt, an Issey Miyake shirt, an Yves Saint Laurent vest, Paul Smith cotton shorts or Kiminori Morishita organza briefs (two for a lari); also, an albino crocodile leather belt by Michael Kors, or Brunello Cucinelli socks, blue with red diamonds. All this stuff is just lying about in the Didube secondhand shops—to say nothing of Lanvin shirts, Missoni scarves, Pal Zileri shirts, Prada boots, Krizia shoes (they price them at ten but will sell for seven) and Nazi-style Dirk Bikkembergs jackets.

It just takes looking through the first few bundles to come across these things.

A Trussardi scarf or a Burberry raincoat; Costume National slippers or an Alexander McQueen hat; Marithé F. Girbaud stockings or a Christian Lacroix robe; a Laura Biagiotti coat or a Cacharel nightcap; an Alessandro Dell'Acqua suit or a Dsquared2 sweater; a Givenchy night dress or a Roberto Cavalli cloak—all this is available. Each bundle contains an agreeable surprise. There really is no end to the Anna Sui jackets, the Ermenegildo Zegna suits, the John Richmond jerseys, the Karl Lagerfeld polos, and the Tom Ford gloves—to say nothing of Tod's moccasins (those horrors have their fans, too)—Sonia Rykiel slippers, Ann Demeulemeester sandals, agnès b. espadrilles, and Lucien Pellat-Finet leaf-patterned sneakers—piles of them. There are so many Cerruti 1881 T-shirts, Marc Jacobs jackets, Donna Karan tops, Emanuel Ungaro slacks, Antonio Marras bags, Balenciaga caps, Pianegonda sandals, and Bally shoes that shop owners are at a loss for what to do with them all. The number of Versace ties here is absolutely sufficient to hang a small nation, say Serbia, from a tree.

Dior? Of course! It simply dominates in Didube. And second-rate goods by such brands as Guess, Zara, and Sisley just lie about in random heaps.

It's true that you might find just one Chanel boot, or the zipper on a pair of Dolce&Gabbana jeans might need to be repaired, but that's beside the point. After all, you can put the boot on one foot and a Yohji Yamamoto shoe on the other. It's your unique style. If the zipper needs to be repaired, fix it with a safety pin; nobody will even notice.

It's worth running a little experiment just to prove it to yourself; all you have to do is enter the first shop where "Brand-New Swedish Bundles" is written on a small piece of cardboard on the door. This is more of a strategic trick to scare away undesirables rather than a real advertisement. The fact is, there's nothing Swedish whatsoever in those shops.

The female shop assistant will glance at you for a second out of the corner of her eye, and then forget about you immediately. *Nil admirari.* She is dressed modestly, given the treasure she owns. Nothing excessive. A true drug dealer never consumes his own stuff. She has a slightly puffed up, alcoholic but intelligent face, with large black circles under her eyes, just like a koala bear has. She is a former breast physician, a homoeopathist, or even an Orientalist. And it's really no marvel, because every other cab driver in Tbilisi is a former teacher, academic secretary, or professional athlete. Behind the shop assistant are a few small paper icons and a calendar pushpinned to the wall. From the calendar, Saakashvili grins so broadly that you'd think he was conducting an advertising campaign for Blend-A-Med toothpaste. His photoshopped teeth are perfectly white. You come across things like that now and then in new issues of the *Sunday Palette*. Ever since the Rose Revolution, Saakashvili has been irremovable as a weed, indelible as ink, inescapable as advertising, and as ubiquitous as döner kebab stands—I mean it's citywide. I stare at the calendar and realize that the photo is quite innocuous, and, most importantly, it's perfectly well-timed. There's no caption or slogan. Just a Google-searched photo framed by roses. The picture, it's true, is photoshopped—the roses are lit up on one side, the president on the other. The overall message still works, though. In this case, the effect of minimalism is especially important given the intellectual, social, and moral context. I keep staring and it dawns on me that precisely *this kind* of commander in chief is needed during wars—the kind who will fight tooth and nail to protect each and every one of his own troops. Only a chief smiles that way, a chief within inches of being canonized as a saint. He has already become superman, though there's nothing behind it all but madness and lightning. The shop assistant has a newspaper spread out on the table; a small TV set sitting on the newspaper shows black-and-white stills of military helicopters. "... Russian military helicopters have just bombed the area around Gagarin Square and Saburtalo Market. The helicopters reportedly used artillery shells and cluster bombs prohibited by the Geneva Conventions. Several houses have been completely destroyed ..." At the same time, a volley of gunfire, followed by an explosion, is heard. The girl cuts bread with a knife. Two eggs are boiling in a small pan on an electric stove. The only source of light in the shop is a single bulb hanging loosely from a gray wire that comes down from the ceiling. The row of swollen bundles shine with Lycra, silver buttons, and organza, resembling slimy alien eggs from the movie *Aliens*. The shop smells of moist rot and the specific, sweetly sour stink of chemical detergent, as if a shower gel-foamed hobo lies behind the bundles. Now begins a long but pleasant process: fumbling through. Experts know that the really good stuff is inside the bundles, rather than on hangers.

After fumbling in the first bundle for ten seconds, a black Fendi sweater with a big white F on the chest comes out. There is a small hole in the left corner of the chest, though. But so what? You can sew a red diamond over the hole, and then place another diamond on the right side, for symmetry. That's the long and the short of it. However, clothes with logos are long out of fashion. When it comes to sweaters, a Dries Van Noten (thick-knit and cream-colored), or this pretty blue Comme des Garçons (with a sateen, egg yolk hem on the right sleeve) are definitely better, even though they both need a good wash. This white Maison Martin Margiela jacket is all right as well. Right here is a very handsome Hermès leather bag; it's absolutely no problem at all that it lacks a shoulder strap. Under the bag, there's AJ denim and a pair of stylishly distressed, vintage-style Helmut Lang jeans. These two pairs don't even need to be compared; the Lang are infinitely better in all respects. They might be a little too distressed, but they're still better. Most importantly, the Lang jeans are sewn with silvery thread. Here's a pair of black John Galliano trousers with black stripes, the knees looking shabby. Big deal! Just cut off the legs and you'll have a perfect pair of shorts. Next comes an Yves Saint Laurent shirt—ninety-eight percent cotton, two-percent Lycra— with a V-shaped neckline, and a pale lemon Masatomo polo that's missing a sleeve. But put a jacket over it and nobody will figure it out. Look at this white Sophia Kokosalaki belt; nobody cares that it's for women; the size is XL. Don't worry that the buckle has no tongue. Complaining about the tongue is the last thing you should do here. And don't shrink from Bresciani socks with shabby heels; nobody will notice your sock heels so long as you're wearing shoes. When the ankles of your socks are all right, the heels are not even with thinking about. This narrow, red-and-green-striped diesel-colored Thierry Mugler scarf is not worth deliberating over either, all the more so because there's nothing wrong with it; perhaps the fringe just needs a little clipping. However, we keep on fumbling anyway. A dark-blue Viktor&Rolf blazer with a blue velvet collar, the stitch falling apart at the shoulder, surfaces next; but, as if in compensation, this Haider Ackermann unisex hat is absolutely ship-shape—only the brims are a little cracked. A smidge of starch will take care of that. Here is a black Kenzo T-shirt bearing an interesting legend:

KENZO ● KONEZ

Since "konez" means "the end" in Russian, perhaps the fashion apocalypse is just around the corner?

This completely brand-new Brioni suit might be twenty years old, but Brioni is so classic, you'll never know which collection it comes from. It's definitely Brioni, not Benetton. Here is a single python skin glove by Gianfranco Ferré. You could put it on one hand and pretend that the other is in the pocket, but who wears Ferré anymore? On the other hand, this kamikaze pilot-style leather jacket by Junya Watanabe, with yellow-tinted Alain Mikli aviators already in the breast pocket, will come perfectly in handy. Also coming in handy is this Jeremy Scott deer skin wallet imprinted with the designer's initials . . . and that synthetic jacket by Blaak, with six buttons and a white dragon embroidered on the left sleeve. Who cares that the glass Evian bottle Jean Paul Gaultier designed is empty? As everybody knows, the bottle is what matters, not the liquid inside it. All the more so since this liquid was only water, even if it was the water of life. Here comes a dark Kris Van Assche blouse with narrow, light-blue lines, and a black Hussein Chalayan overcoat in a perfect condition. (Although, the overcoat has belt straps but no actual belt.) Nevertheless, you know that Arthur on Silver Street can make a belt for this overcoat so similar that nobody would ever make out where the belt was manufactured—in some top fashion factory in Milan, or in Arthur's tiny apartment. Therefore, the only remaining question is whether we should purchase the Chalayan overcoat, or the hooded, dark-khaki tweed manteau with wide pockets by Etro. These Hedi Slimane sneakers don't even need to be checked; all you have to do is glue the soles and get some laces.

So:

The bag (Hermès) – 10 L
The sweater (Comme des Garçons) – 8 L
The T-shirt (Kenzo) – 2 L
The jacket (Blaak) – 5 L
The jeans (Helmut Lang) – 9 L
The trousers (John Galliano) – 8 L
The polo (Masatomo) – 3 L
The belt (Sophia Kokosalaki) – 2 L
The scarf (Thierry Mugler) – 1.5 L
The hat (Haider Ackermann) – 2 L

The blazer (Viktor&Rolf) – 9 L
The jacket (Junya Watanabe) + glasses (Alain Mikli) – 10 L
The wallet (Jeremy Scott) – 0.5 L
The blouse (Kris Van Assche) – 4 L
The bottle (Jean Paul Gaultier for Evian) – 0.2 L
The overcoat (Hussein Chalayan) – 30 L
The shoes (Hedi Slimane for Dior Homme) – 10 L
Total: 114.2 L

Anyway, don't get too carried away. This stuff is now yours for good. Don't forget, though, that you've got to drop by Arthur's to have the belt made. You've also got to get your shoes glued, among other things. From the TV comes the voice of a newscaster: "... Georgia's Foreign Ministry appeals to the international community to strongly protest the actions of Russia within the territory of Georgia, urging Russia to cease military operations. The statement by Georgia's Foreign Ministry ..." While you calculate the total in your mind, the shop assistant turns the volume off, takes the eggs out of the pot, and tells you what you expect: "A hundred laris for everything." She even puts a pair of Bresciani socks—as a gift—on your pile, while peeling the egg with her other hand. It still sounds expensive though; a hundred laris doesn't grow on trees. Then immediately it dawns on you that in the aforementioned boutiques of Vere and Vake, they wouldn't even fart at you for a hundred laris; moreover, all you could get for this price in a market is just a pair of adibas sneakers.

13. SOME THIRD ALTERNATIVE

For twenty minutes now, Tika and I have been lounging under a canopy on the veranda of the Kopala hotel, waiting for Keira and Carlos. They're still in their suite. I'm in a perfect mood. Not just because Carlos is a nice guy, and not just because I'm sure that he brought Bolivian marching powder. I'm just in a perfect mood, for no reason at all. I want to think positively about something good. Nothing comes to mind though, only meaningless fragments that don't make any sense at all. Meanwhile, my thoughts drift to Georgian villages with pointedly non-Georgian sounding names, and where the hell those names might have come from. Take, for example, *Bushet* in Kakheti, *Gostibe* in Kaspi, the sublimely poetic *Zhebota* in Tianeti, or the Japanese-sounding *Akura* in the Telavi municipality.

The waitress puts our drinks down on the table.

"Would you like anything else?"

I sip iced tea.

"Not yet," Tika smiles at her. "Thank you."

The waitress smiles back, too. Then she nods her head in such a strange way that it's hard to say whether she's really nodding or she isn't, and leaves us.

Almost the whole of Tbilisi is spread before our eyes. Metekhi, the Mtkvari, a part of Leselidze Street, and Narikala in particular. You can feel the sickly heat billowing up from the city. I hear helicopters humming somewhere behind us. The wind blows imperceptibly. Hot and cool masses of air blend lazily. It's nice to be on the Kopala veranda at this time of a day.

"Keira has come," Tika told me in the morning.

"Keira?" I was surprised. "When?"

"Six A.M."

"Alone?"

"With Carlos."

That was different. All I ever hear about is Stass, alias Carlos—Keira's husband, and a fantastic guy. If nothing else, all the coke we coolly snorted this past spring in Moscow was directly or indirectly connected to Carlos. Carlos is just like a Somali pirate—you haven't seen him, but you've heard a lot. *Carlos's coke . . . Is this Carlos's coke? . . . Carlos's coke, super . . . Give Carlos a buzz . . .*

I've seen the mythical Carlos himself just once. However, it was at such close range, and I was so stoned, that I fail to remember the guy's face. I was in the john at the exclusive Moscow club Krysha Mira. The line of coke he put on the screen of his Vertu was so thick that I thought he was trying to kill me. All I remember is that he's one head shorter than me, has a doughy complexion, and his hair is highlighted and gelled, just like a former boy band member. Carlos kind of sparkles and shines all over, not just because his diamond Boucheron cufflinks and porcelain teeth glisten under light. He emits beams of his own from out his eyes: *I am the superman, and I consider nothing that is the superman's to be alien to me.* Carlos uses exquisite cologne. The fragrance always sort of rings a bell; I mean, it urges you to recall something to mind. Eventually you fail to distinguish what cologne it is or what it reminds you of.

"Take it," he told me, and handed me a golden snorting straw.

I remember that straw better than Carlos himself. Weird, luminescent letters ran along the side, just like the ring from the trilogy *The Lord of the Rings*. As soon as I got what I was supposed to get, I immediately noticed that Carlos was a nice guy; he even had a sense of humor, which is very rare among such rich people. I'm not sure whether he made it up himself or was just repeating somebody else's words, but he told me that evening that for rich Russians like him, vodka should be especially bottled with a label like this:

LUXURY VODKA

That's what he drew with his index fingertip on the glass pane of the steamed-up door in the john.

Perhaps there are some people who, even if they drink tanks of vintage French wine or cognac while simultaneously consuming piles of Bolivian powder, still remain vodka men; maybe good vodka men—but who cares?

As for Keira, she has all it takes to be a good woman, too. As long as you have designer dresses exclusively made for cocktail parties, plus your own massage therapist, you have to try hard to be bad. Keira and Tika are childhood friends; nevertheless, they went their separate ways after Keira married Carlos and moved to London, and they haven't been as close ever since. To think that before they were inseparable in a Thelma and Louise kind of way. The way I figure it, it's not just that Keira's perception of the world changed sharply and unexpectedly. I mean, the world itself changed for *her*. It's like she can't get a full sense of what's happening, so wherever she is—Tokyo, Rio, or The Maldives—she keeps on making phone calls to Tika. She can't live without Tika.

"Why are they taking so long?" Tika looks down at her cell phone.

"Go for it," I urge her. "Call her."

"You mean . . ."

"I mean, find out where the hell they need to be for so long."

"I will in five minutes."

I can't get the hang of the subtleties of *five minutes*. Tika handles time her own way. I'm not sure that I'll ever find out the true reasons behind her coming to an appointment ten minutes late—or arriving thirty minutes early for a movie. The list goes on. And it's also unlikely that I'll ever learn what extraordinary thing or act of God urged Keira to come to Tbilisi today especially, in the middle of a war. It obviously wasn't missing Tika. It's got to be something else.

Behind Tika sits a puny little guy two tables away, dressed in blue trousers, white sneakers, and white, low-cut socks. He's got a bald head, a crooked bird-like nose, and a tiny, old-man-like double chin. From where I sit, I can't make out the newspaper he's reading; all I can see is that it's some foreign edition. He seems like a handsome, well-tended old timer, ready for a coffin. A touristy-looking group of Dutch reporters sits to his right, five of them: three men and two women, each holding a good camera. They somehow manage to make a quiet sort of noise discussing where to go first, the mortuary or the hospital. If I heard right, yesterday their fellow reporters, a certain Storimans and Akkermans of RTL Nieuws, were injured in the Gori bombing. However, it's not clear which one of them is in the morgue and which is in the hospital. At times I make eye contact with one of the women; she has lilac hair. She must be between twenty and twenty-five; a coffee and a small plate with half a piece of cake on it are placed before her.

The phone starts to vibrate on the table. Tika looks down at the screen.

"That Keira?" I inquire.

Tika says no with a shake of her head. "Bobo," she answers.

Before she speaks again, Bobo rushes immediately to my mind. To be more exact, her firm nipples, slender waistline, and the piercing in her navel—a tiny platinum embryo. Bobo and I broke up around this time last summer. Not because of Tika. However, I did meet Tika through Bobo. Anyway, you could say that somehow we didn't jive together very well. Her blow job is still tops though. Even Tika can't suck the way she does.

Tika puts the cell phone to her ear. "Yeah, Bobo?"

Keira gives lousy head. I don't get what Carlos digs about her. It so happened that earlier this spring in the very same Krysha Mira, my dick somehow found itself in Keira's mouth. It was her, not me. Stealthily she led me to the john, leaned me against the wall, squatted, and pulled my pants down. I felt somewhat embarrassed to turn her down. I was so pumped up but blissed out at the same time from Carlos's hit that I wouldn't have turned down my own mother. All the manual-oral stuff got a rise out of me, but to no avail—Keira's enthusiasm turned off equally fast. I couldn't even cum. The blow job was no big deal either. Eventually, overwhelmed by Valium, Keira ended up almost asleep on my dick.

I know Keira's Cinderella story almost by heart. An absolutely second-rate artist who gobbled a handful of Valium a day and painted ridiculously small pictures because she was scared to waste oil paints, Keira suddenly got into protecting animals' rights, parroting slogans, and having orgasms—as she tells it—in her own Ferrari. Perhaps she's still gobbling Valium, but for totally different reasons now. Reasons are what really matter. So, I do wonder what inspired her to come to Tbilisi specifically today, in the heat of the war. It's extremely out of character for Keira to do anything just for the hell of it, all the more so because she hasn't been in Tbilisi for five years. It's not like Muhammad going to the mountain or vice versa. It's some third alternative: where Muhammad and the mountain meet on neutral territory. Like the way Napoleon and Alexander I met on neutral territory—a specially prepared raft in the middle of the Neman River on June

25, 1807. Maybe today, August 8, 2008, the Kopala veranda of Kopala is like the Neman, a sort of a portal into parallel worlds for Tika and Keira?

Besides, no matter however many animals' rights Keira protects, however well her Chinese massage therapist massages her, however many orgasms she has at a time with Carlos (and not only with him), or however often she wipes her ass with Chanel toilet paper, deep down at a molecular level she's the same old Keira she ever was: a flat-chested girl from Nutsubidze, making miniature paintings.

She probably feels insecure about her past, though; that's perhaps why she keeps calling from different places—it's a way to escape herself. As far as I know, Tika doesn't give a fuck about all that stuff. She couldn't care less if Keira called her from a Ferrari or the Nutsubidze slums, if she's wearing a one-of-a-kind dress or her old pink top where her pointed, low-hanging nipples constantly showed through. So I figure that's their friendship and the mutual closeness she cherishes. At times she's very sweet and sentimental. Perhaps all these changing things in Keira's life are crappy entertainment in some way. Though I, too, wish I were in Maldives right now, if only to buzz my best buddies from my own yacht.

It's just hard not to feel overwhelmed by emotion, all the more so when you're slowly sipping piña coladas while lying in a hammock strung between palm trees and enjoying the summer sunset, a necklace of flowers around your neck and the ocean breeze gently caressing your face.

My cell phone rings. An unknown number blinks on the screen.

"Hello, Shako, is that you?" a familiar voice asks.

"Yeah, speaking."

"Shako, it's Nugo here." A pause follows. "From *Sarke*."

The name tells me nothing. Instead, the squeak of his voice reminds me of Father Elias.

"How are you, Nugo?" I inquire.

"Good." A pause. "Are you in Tbilisi?"

"Yes."

"Listen! Georgian Pepsi wants to shoot you in a commercial."

I don't know how I should react to this. It's ridiculous even to talk seriously about any success whatsoever in Georgia. Yet, it's pleasant to know that Pepsi wants you for a commercial, which means you unknowingly fit all stereotypes currently in demand.

"Great," I reply. "Photo or video?"

"I'll explain in person." Another pause. "Could we meet as soon as today?"

"Today?" I think into the cell phone. "Actually yes."

"On Sharden at four? Is that okay with you?"

I want to reply that it's not. That I go to Antalya the day after tomorrow. However, Sharden sounds promising. I mean, they'll probably pay well. I'm also aware that the level will be *totally* different. That is, Tbilisi is not the hub of the world and I am not David Beckham. However, the customer *is* Pepsi, albeit Georgian, and Sharden will remain the same. I mean, everything's costly here, including a primetime commercial. And the costliness is contagious, too. That is, if you allow a stinking bum to enter one end of the shortest of streets, he will come out a sophisticated aesthete at the other end, equally aware of the latest high fashion trends and the various aromas produced by exclusive cigars. It really does happen. To be more precise, every other man on Sharden Street is a former bum ready to leave directly for the catwalks of Paris, London, and Milan. Luxury suits, collagen lips, and porcelain teeth mingle together. Here you'll always come across local politicians, Telman the barber, or Bubba with his charming smile, not to mention celebrities. Even the president might drop by unexpectedly. Why not? It's accepted in small countries. Besides, where there is Bubba, there is the president: and vice versa: where there's the president, there's Bubba. It's hard at times to understand which of the two is president and which is Bubba. President–Bubba. *Hubba-Bubba.*

"On Sharden," I answer. "At four."

The Dutch woman behind Tika stands up. She wears very small, artificially torn jean shorts, a white top, and white moccasins. A diamond ring shines in her navel. I stare at her long legs. Her top shows that she's not wearing a bra. Her moderately sized breasts shake slightly. Her short, lavender hair gleams neon against the whiteness of her untanned body. Her body is slender, just like Violet's in the movie *Ultraviolet.*

"Agreed?" Nugo wants to make sure.

I'm aware of the horny way I'm behaving, but I can't take my eyes off her. But she doesn't stop looking either. She gazes straight into my eyes and smiles weirdly. We keep on staring at each other. If Tinto Brass and Sergio Leone had ever filmed an erotic western together, they would have undoubtedly included a similar scene: wide shot/close-up/wide shot/close-up/eyes/ eyes . . . The background music would be like early Morricone. Charles Bronson plays harmonica. However, post-*Matrix* slow motion, a rotating camera, and a bullet time effect would also work. This whole eye contact thing lasts just for a couple seconds. Tika doesn't notice. The Dutch woman leaves the veranda. She doesn't take her gaze off me until the glass door shuts. I gaze back at her. Like an expert at ESP. I can't tell whether we've reached telepathic consensus or not. I don't know either whether she got irritated by my behavior or was pleased in some respect.

"Agreed." I put the phone down on the table.

"I'll call you back in the evening," says Tika to Bobo. "All right? See you."

She hangs up.

"Who was that?" she asks.

"Nugo," I reply, "from *Sarke.*"

"Nugo?" Tika shrugs her shoulders. "What did he want?"

"Pepsi wants me in its commercial."

Tika's cell phone rings. She looks down at the screen. "It's Keira," she tells me, then puts the phone to her ear.

"Keira?"

Nugo calls me again. "Yeah, Nugo," I reply.

"Just heard the report that Sharden is blocked."

The squeal of Nugo's voice remind me of Father Elias again—a nice guy and an absolute surprise when it comes to the Georgian Orthodox Church. He was an embodied antibody. Last year, a couple other guys and I accidentally found ourselves in his cell in the Gremi church in eastern Georgia. An impromptu table was set, with only honey vodka and food for breaking the fast. Eventually, Father Elias ended up calling one of his parishioners on his cell phone and having him bring down a karaoke machine. As a dessert, the Father performed for us Britney's "Toxic" with such gusto that I almost believed in God. It's not that he reacted this way because of the alcohol. He just turned out to be a groovy kind of guy, and his message was that we were the same. In this fashion, he showed respect for us. He remained cheerful and vivacious right to the end. Nevertheless, his eyes were somewhat sad and over-tired. It must've been a long way for him from spermatozoid to the act of contrition.

"I can't see it from here," I tell Nugo, turning my neck at the same time so I can see what's going on Sharden. A really cyberpunkish picture: A herd of bicyclists rides along the highway. They look tired, bending forward in their seats and pushing the pedals heavily. Due to their egg-shaped helmets, reflective glasses, and aerodynamic suits—which stick to their bodies—they look like sci-fi movie characters. A gray Ford Sierra drives behind the herd. With this, Father Elias comes to mind again: his black robe, a cross around his neck, a microphone in hand, and tired eyes.

"Imedi reported Sharden blocked by troops," says Nugo.

The city is clearly visible from the veranda. I feel rather than see that something is not the way it was just a moment ago . . . something has changed. You have to know Tbilisi well to feel these shifts. Tbilisi is as soft and obedient as modeling clay, a hyperrealistic city. Anyone can model it, color it, rape it at will, and, most importantly, fake it. It asks you, orders you, and addresses you directly to color it, to rape it, and to fake it. But if it depended on me, at each entrance to the city I'd hang banners with the message FAKE ME rather than COLOR ME or FUCK ME. FUCK ME is the very message which, from my point of view, specifically manifests the heart, soul, and spirit of this city. Especially now. Besides, a war has its own language: short, sharp, and easy to remember; just like the way the Russian-Chechen wartime reports forever preserved online two corny banners hung at the gates of Grozny at different times. The first banner read WELCOME TO HELL. Later, the second banner appeared: WELCOME TO HELL: PART II. It looked like a scene from Kitano's *Dolls*. Sometimes the particular lines you remember from movies are so appealing, you forget to even care what the plot was.

If you bear in mind that Tbilisi is the most Armenian city, as more Armenians live here than in Yerevan, and that nearly every successful Georgian has at least an Armenian grandmother, then at the gates of Tbilisi we could hang a banner like this:

EMPORIO ⩔ ARMENI

"Super," Tika says to Keira.

"What should we do?" I ask Nugo.

Through the glass panes I catch a glimpse of a TV screen fixed to a wall. An elderly woman with a blood-stained face lies on the ground in front of a burning house and thrusts out her hands helplessly toward the camera; nearby is a flipped Red Cross van and a small burning bus with charred wheels. A Bronze Stalin stands intact in the middle of the shot. It seems they're showing Gori. It's the only place on earth where a statue of the great chief still stands. Somewhere in the background, a soldier, bent forward, runs away while shooting a machine gun. The news ticker in the lower part of the screen reads: ". . . open a deposit account before December 16 in TBC Bank and win one out of 10 Mercedes or the main prize of 1,000,000 laris. Become a millionaire with TBC Bank! . . ."

A military pilot probably doesn't care whether he bombs a city, a forest, or a chicken coop. All he can see from his altitude are buildings and targets: a pretty dry scene. Would I feel anything if I were a pilot pushing a bomb button? And, moreover, if I knew that I was bombing Zhebota, Gostibe, or Bushet?

"Okay!" Tika tells Keira, and then turns her phone off.

"Let me make sure first. I'll call you back," Nugo tells me. "Okay?"

"Okay," I reply. "I'll wait."

I put the cell phone on the table.

"So what about Keira?" I ask Tika.

"She wants us to drop by for a while."

"Great." I sip my tea. That means Carlos's got Bolivian powder on him.

14. THOUGHT ON THE
RIVERSIDE OF MTKVARI II/
ZONE REALITY

We could have lived through
We could have killed through
We could have kissed through
We could have missed through

We could have loved through
We could have laughed through
We could have fucked through
We could have sucked through

We could have slept through
We could have rapped through
We could have helped through
We could have begged through

We could have reigned through
We could have played through
We could have prayed through
We could have brayed through

We could have named through
We could have gamed through
We could have faked through
We could have raged through

We could have written through
We could have bitten through
We could have beaten through
We could have eaten through

We could have snoozed through
We could have boozed through
We could have grooved through
We could have googled through

We could have dropped through
We could have blogged through
We could have bombed through
We could have walked through

We could have drugged through
We could have parked through
We could have asked through
We could have masked through

We could have doped through
We could have posed through
We could have dosed through
We could have closed through

We could have assed through
We could have blessed through
We could have dressed through
We could have pressed through

We could have bitched through
We could have pinched through
We could have fixed through
We could have mixed through

We could have fleeced through
We could have sniffed through
We could have peed through
We could have healed through

We could have starved through
We could have snubbed through
We could have hummed through
We could have chuckled through

We could have braked through
We could have freaked through
We could have feasted through
We could have shat through

We could have thought through
We could have sold through
We could have bossed through
We could have crossed through

We could have rested through
We could have arrested through
We could have plugged through
We could have unplugged through

We could have spoiled through
We could have boiled through
We could have courted through
We could have counted through

We could have involved through
We could have injured through
We could have mused through
We could have amused through

We could have massaged through
We could have managed through
We could have protested through
We could have protected through

We could have distorted through
We could have deported through
We could have reported through
We could have recorded through

We could have replayed through
We could have x-rayed through
We could have retired through
We could have required through

We could have realized through
We could have recognized through
We could have minimized through
We could have maximized through

We could have hypnotized through
We could have brutalized through
We could have memorized through
We could have terrorized through

We could have buried through
We could have pussied through
We could have fasted through
We could have chatted through

We could have soaped through
We could have foamed through
We could have clowned through
We could have flown through

We could have shaken through
We could have taken through
We could have outdone through
We could have overdone through

We could have panicked through
We could have punished through
We could have puzzled through
We could have dazzled through

We could have voted through
We could have devoted through
We could have formed through
We could have performed through

We could have excused through
We could have seduced through
We could have confused through
We could have confessed through

We could have exported through
We could have imported through
We could have mended through
We could have melted through

We could have swallowed through
We could have followed through
We could have borrowed through
We could have sorrowed through

We could have appeared through
We could have appealed through
We could have measured through
We could have gathered through

We could have discoursed through
We could have discounted through
We could have lounged through
We could have scrounged through
—more proudly.

15. NOTHING SPECIAL

I come out of the bathroom, wrapping a towel around my waist. I hear Tako's voice from the living room. She must be talking on Skype. I clean my ear with a cotton swab. Then I look through the open window into the yard. Two guys from my block sit on the street curb next to an old Moskvich on bricks. Just regular Tbilisians—neither hardened gangsters nor hardened dope fiends. Being absolutely good for nothing, they work to create the illusion of being very busy. One texts on his cell phone while the other scratches something on the Moskvich door.

Black smoke comes from somewhere. Someone's beating a rug with a stick on one of the balconies. Some children play soccer on a playground. TVs are heard through the open windows: "... people who have lost their homes will be provided with food products and articles of daily necessity..."

I come into the living room. Tako lies on the sofa, on her side—the only pose in Georgian yoga. She's talking to Naniko through Skype. She doesn't look sexy at all. I mean that lying on her side doesn't suit her. She rests in peace more than she lies, frigidity emanating from her body and soul.

"What does it say on TV?" Naniko asks.

"I don't know." Tako yawns. "Haven't turned it on yet."

"News reports here say that Tbilisi may be subject to chemical attacks, and that embassies are leaving the city."

"Hold on. I'll turn it on." Tako cranes her neck, looking around.

"Looking for the remote control?" I ask.

"Yeah. You see it anywhere?"

On the table there's a laptop, Tako's cell phone, and the July issue of *GQ* half-covered by an empty Scriabin's Donuts paper bag and a bottle of Actimel.

"How are you, Gio?" Naniko greets me from the screen.

"Fine," I tell her. "How's Molko doing?"

I put cotton swabs into the bottle of Actimel.

"You kidding?" She pouts her collagen lips in a contrived way, looking sort of hurt.

Her talentless artistry cheers me up.

"Stay fake," I tell her.

"What you mean?" she asks.

"Forget it." I answer. "Can't find the remote control," I tell Tako.

She looks around goose-like. Then she puts her hand in between the pillows.

I feel a hard-on slowly coming on. That's just like Tako—the more relaxed she is, the hornier you get. I know how to unlock her reserves of energy. I drop to my knees by the sofa and start massaging Tako's back, her boyish-looking shoulders.

"What're you doing?" she asks me, and lazily stretches back across the sofa, purring cat-like.

"Relax," I tell her, but it's absolutely unnecessary. She can't relax any more than she already has. I feel her becoming a jellyfish. Just thinking about any sort of massage turns her brain on, and she becomes impulsive like a psycho, then soft and submissive as modeling clay. It's true though that my manual maneuvers have less to do with Thai or Shiatsu techniques and more with the mere imitation of massage. Nevertheless it's perfectly sufficient to drive Tako crazy. Her hair gives off this just-woken-up warm smell. I start to take her T-shirt off, caressing her nipples. Shivers from pleasure run all down her spine. She sneaks her hand under my towel and touches my cock.

I take her shorts off. She raises her legs up, helping me pull her g-string off. Her nipples are hard. Naniko keeps quiet, carefully watching us from the screen. She is delicately silent, realizing she should keep a low profile at the moment. I spread Tako's legs wide apart. A tiny triangle sits on her pubic area—the trace of her bathing suit. Naniko keeps a watchful eye on Tako's vagina, as if expecting a bird to fly out from inside. I start very gently, touching her rosy clit with the tip of my tongue. I lick the oily lips as her knees shiver slightly.

All of a sudden Tako sits up on the sofa and removes my towel.

"Lie down," she tells me.

I obey without a word. She sits on my face, licks my cock, then wets her index finger and starts to tickle my sphincter. I feel her finger reach halfway up my anal passage. I bite her swollen clit with my front teeth. I love any kind of vagina: clipped, hairy, shaved, pierced, tattooed . . . even in the "critical" days, particularly close to the end—that is, when the menstrual flow changes color from dogwood-pink to Ferrari-red, a truly Italian red—*rosso corsa*. My love for vagina sits deep on a molecular level in my heart. The main point is that it's supposed to be pretty and well-groomed. My brain is permanently connected to this image, just the way a personal computer is connected to the global network. What I like best of all is Tako's vagina. It's already turned into my au-topilot, my Shangri-la, my language, my motherland, my faith. The minute it sees me, its petal lips open up and spread out in an inviting sort of way. Just like the ninth gate from the movie *The Ninth Gate*. This is the eternal call. Tako is eternally ready for me. That's what really freaks me out and screws my brain up. At moments like this, I'm just meat, happy meat at that.

There's a similar scene in an Almodovar movie: as the result of a weird experiment, a man shrinks so small that he can go into his sweetheart's pussy. If I could, I would go headlong inside Tako like a mole.

The clean-shaven pubic bone bites my nose. Her vagina oozes so much fluid that I hardly have time to swallow it. I gently chew her clit.

"Would you get on all fours for a bit?" I ask her.

Then I spread her cheeks wide apart and pass my tongue along her rosy, coffee-with-milk sphincter. It contracts reflexively and then slowly relaxes. Contracts and then relaxes . . . just like a flower during accelerated filming. I wet it with my saliva. Color sparkles shine from the wet wrinkles the way a sunray shines around the facets of a diamond.

She doesn't seem to like this particularly. Therefore, I enter her anally as slowly as I can. She reflexively squeezes my cock with her sphincter. I fondle her nipples with my fingers. I maintain eye contact with Naniko. She carefully watches us from the screen, trying not to miss a thing.

I think involuntarily about whether today's date could mean anything more than its calendar value. What could 08/08/08 mean? Could it mean infinity nullified and raised to the third power, due to the resemblance between 8 and ∞? The resemblance between eight and an hourglass probably also means something: 0⧗/0⧗/0⧗. What about nullified time raised to the third power? And if we arrange these numbers vertically, so that zero is below eight, and concentrate hard, we see a man with an open mouth: the eight makes his eyes, the zero his mouth. Rather, it's a toothless man. That's not the point though. The point here is that he's toothless and shouting. Nevertheless, we've got to know the reason that's making him shout. And things like the eight planets of the solar system, the eight doors of heaven in Islam, the eight times eight squares on chessboards, and the eight noble paths of Buddhism only matter if the zero in this given case is a neutral element, and just during addition and subtraction at that. All other mathematical operations would only nullify, that is, *pussify*, in some ways, any given number. A vagina as a perfect zero. And vice versa. By the way, Wikipedia could have answered all this for us and saved me the trouble. And last but not least, if we assume that the eight is a pair of testicles, and the zero is a vagina, then it becomes clear why a penis is nowhere to be seen. It is already in the vagina. Does this mean that 08 is a symbol for sex? Based on this logic, we may tie today's date to the ongoing war—at least, we can do so insofar as the war itself is an imitation of sex, or, on the contrary, sex is an imitation of the war. I feel on the verge of cumming.

"I'm gonna cum," I tell Tako.

"Don't stop."

"What about you?"

"Go on!"

Tako's cell phone rings, its screen and keyboard shining like phosphorus. It starts to crawl and vibrate along the table: *bz-zzzzz*. Nokia's original ringtone is heard; it's like choral singing. Tako lies on her stomach as I withdraw my cock from inside her.

"Answer, please," says Tako, and lies back on the pillow.

I look down at the screen. It's Sopo Rusadze. Before I answer, it suddenly occurs to me that Sopo is a good reporter. Her show on the First Channel is the only one that I can watch without disgust. I like everything about Sopo—the way she dresses, thinks, talks . . . The only thing I can't dig is that she drives a black Toyota Prado, just like Tbilisi goons do. I think that car is too much for a woman. When speaking of Sopo, it's hard not to remember the movie *Drunken Master*. I'm talking about that kung fu strategy where a fighter *pretends to be drunk*. In Sopo's case, the whole bottom line is that she never pretends. Furthermore, she always tries hard to stay in the big picture, but, high on tranquilizers, it often takes her a few seconds to catch the meaning of what's been said.

If it were up to me, I'd have only attractive, sexy women working as reporters, just like on Italian TV channels; you never know whether a newscaster is a photo model or a Brazilian beach volleyball team member. I mean, I wouldn't want to be interviewed by some talking toad; no greetings from the water world. With the exception of sirens, I haven't yet gotten it up for any erudite swamp things. Besides, you naturally try to charm a reporter who attracts you physically, and furthermore, manages your emotions in the right way. And you always try to make each of your answers better than the last. And it's not just the answers. I mean, at the end of the interview you shouldn't feel like you've just been fucked by an intellectual frog, jellyfish, or amphibian.

Before I manage to say hello, Sopo asks me in a sleepy voice, "Gio, is that you?"

"Oh yesss," I answer. "How are you, babe?"

She ignores my question.

"Where's Tako?"

"In the bathroom. Anything urgent?"

"Just don't tell her . . ." a pause follows. "I had a bad dream about her."

"What was the dream about?" I ask.

"Nothing special."

She wouldn't have called just because of *nothing special.*

"Tell me!" I insist.

"She's alive. That's all that matters," she says, and abruptly goes quiet. I think I hear her yawning.

The silence stretches on. "Sopo?"

". . ."

Did she fall asleep or were we disconnected? I keep looking at the phone, trying at the same time to guess what, in Sopo's view, is a bad dream, or what she could have seen in her dream. Some maniac biting Tako's nipples off, cutting her fingers off with a garden pruner, boring her ankles through, and plucking her eyes out with a spoon? I wonder what she watched before going to bed—the latest news, or some Mexican TV series?

"Was that Rusadze?" Tako asks me. She's still looking for the remote control, rummaging through the pillows.

"Yeah," I tell her. "She had a bad dream about you."

"Here it is." Tako fishes out the remote control from between the pillows. Then she turns the plasma screen on.

The screen squeals, slowly lighting up. Footage, shot with a cell phone, shows a fighter jet in flames and circling the sky, leaving black clouds of smoke.

"What did she dream up?" Naniko asks from the laptop.

"Nothing special."

TRANSLATOR'S NOTES

p. 16   *Der grüne punkt*: "The green dot" is the trademark symbol of German recycling company Duales System Deutschland GmbH.

p. 17   *Eduard Shevardnadze*: Georgia's secretary general under communism (1972–1985), the Soviet foreign minister (1985–1991), and the president of Georgia (1992–2003).

p. 27   *Vint*: Cheap, homemade methamphetamine.

p. 38   *Mangia! Mangia!*: This exhortation, which means "Eat! Eat!" in Italian, recalls the scene from Pier Paolo Pasolini's 1975 film *Salò, or the 120 Days of Sodom*, in which characters are forced to consume their own excrement.

p. 40   *Kakha Kaladze*: A Georgian soccer player.

p. 42   *"Abkhazia is our main trouble"*: A popular, politically charged phrase in Georgia. After the armed conflict in Abkhazia, a disputed territory of Georgia, many ethnic Georgians became refugees.

p. 42   *The Great Yokai War*: A Japanese horror-fantasy film directed by Takashi Miike (2005).

p. 44   *Sarke*: A national magazine famed for yellow journalism.

p. 48   *Chokha*: A traditional Georgian garment worn by men.

p. 66   *Italian yards*: A humorous term for old, shabby houses where several families live together, recalling postwar Italy.

p. 67   *Muntadhar al-Zaidi*: A correspondent of Egyptian-based Al-Baghdadia TV who, during a press conference held for George W. Bush and Iraqi president Nouri al-Maliki in 2008, suddenly jumped up, shouted, "This is a gift from the Iraqis. This is a farewell kiss, you dog!" and threw his shoes at Bush.

p. 77   *Mikheil Saakashvili*: Georgia's third president, elected in 2004.

Zaza Burchuladze, a graduate of Tbilisi State Academy of Arts, has been publishing his stories in Georgian newspapers and magazines since 1998. Regarded in Georgia as a provocative and experimental writer, Burchuladze has also translated the work of Fyodor Dostoyevsky and Daniil Kharms into Georgian. He is a lecturer at the Caucasus Media School.

Guram Sanikidze is a translator based in Georgia.

GEORGIAN LITERATURE SERIES

In 2012, the Ministry of Culture and Monument Protection of Georgia collaborated with Dalkey Archive Press to publish *Contemporary Georgian Fiction*, a landmark anthology providing English-language readers with their first introduction to some of the greatest authors writing in Georgian since the restoration of independence.

Given the success of this project, the relationship between Dalkey Archive and the Ministry has evolved into a close, ongoing partnership, allowing an unprecedented number of translations of the major works of post-Soviet Georgian literature to published and publicized across the English-speaking world. Beginning with such contemporary classics as Aka Morchiladze's best-selling *Journey to Karabakh*, the Georgian Literature Series will provide readers with a much-needed overview of a vibrant and innovative literary culture that has thus far been sorely under-represented in translation.

SELECTED DALKEY ARCHIVE TITLES

MICHAL AJVAZ, *The Golden Age.*
　The Other City.
PIERRE ALBERT-BIROT, *Grabinoulor.*
YUZ ALESHKOVSKY, *Kangaroo.*
FELIPE ALFAU, *Chromos.*
　Locos.
IVAN ÂNGELO, *The Celebration.*
　The Tower of Glass.
ANTÓNIO LOBO ANTUNES, *Knowledge of Hell.*
　The Splendor of Portugal.
ALAIN ARIAS-MISSON, *Theatre of Incest.*
JOHN ASHBERY AND JAMES SCHUYLER, *A Nest of Ninnies.*
ROBERT ASHLEY, *Perfect Lives.*
GABRIELA AVIGUR-ROTEM, *Heatwave and Crazy Birds.*
DJUNA BARNES, *Ladies Almanack.*
　Ryder.
JOHN BARTH, *LETTERS.*
　Sabbatical.
DONALD BARTHELME, *The King.*
　Paradise.
SVETISLAV BASARA, *Chinese Letter.*
MIQUEL BAUÇÀ, *The Siege in the Room.*
RENÉ BELLETTO, *Dying.*
MAREK BIEŃCZYK, *Transparency.*
ANDREI BITOV, *Pushkin House.*
ANDREJ BLATNIK, *You Do Understand.*
LOUIS PAUL BOON, *Chapel Road.*
　My Little War.
　Summer in Termuren.
ROGER BOYLAN, *Killoyle.*
IGNÁCIO DE LOYOLA BRANDÃO,
　Anonymous Celebrity.
　Zero.
BONNIE BREMSER, *Troia: Mexican Memoirs.*
CHRISTINE BROOKE-ROSE, *Amalgamemnon.*
BRIGID BROPHY, *In Transit.*
GERALD L. BRUNS, *Modern Poetry and the Idea of Language.*
GABRIELLE BURTON, *Heartbreak Hotel.*
MICHEL BUTOR, *Degrees.*
　Mobile.
G. CABRERA INFANTE, *Infante's Inferno.*
　Three Trapped Tigers.
JULIETA CAMPOS,
　The Fear of Losing Eurydice.
ANNE CARSON, *Eros the Bittersweet.*
ORLY CASTEL-BLOOM, *Dolly City.*
LOUIS-FERDINAND CÉLINE, *Castle to Castle.*
　Conversations with Professor Y.
　London Bridge.
　Normance.
　North.
　Rigadoon.
MARIE CHAIX, *The Laurels of Lake Constance.*
HUGO CHARTERIS, *The Tide Is Right.*
ERIC CHEVILLARD, *Demolishing Nisard.*

MARC CHOLODENKO, *Mordechai Schamz.*
JOSHUA COHEN, *Witz.*
EMILY HOLMES COLEMAN, *The Shutter of Snow.*
ROBERT COOVER, *A Night at the Movies.*
STANLEY CRAWFORD, *Log of the S.S. The Mrs Unguentine.*
　Some Instructions to My Wife.
RENÉ CREVEL, *Putting My Foot in It.*
RALPH CUSACK, *Cadenza.*
NICHOLAS DELBANCO, *The Count of Concord.*
　Sherbrookes.
NIGEL DENNIS, *Cards of Identity.*
PETER DIMOCK, *A Short Rhetoric for Leaving the Family.*
ARIEL DORFMAN, *Konfidenz.*
COLEMAN DOWELL,
　Island People.
　Too Much Flesh and Jabez.
ARKADII DRAGOMOSHCHENKO, *Dust.*
RIKKI DUCORNET, *The Complete Butcher's Tales.*
　The Fountains of Neptune.
　The Jade Cabinet.
　Phosphor in Dreamland.
WILLIAM EASTLAKE, *The Bamboo Bed.*
　Castle Keep.
　Lyric of the Circle Heart.
JEAN ECHENOZ, *Chopin's Move.*
STANLEY ELKIN, *A Bad Man.*
　Criers and Kibitzers, Kibitzers and Criers.
　The Dick Gibson Show.
　The Franchiser.
　The Living End.
　Mrs. Ted Bliss.
FRANÇOIS EMMANUEL, *Invitation to a Voyage.*
SALVADOR ESPRIU, *Ariadne in the Grotesque Labyrinth.*
LESLIE A. FIEDLER, *Love and Death in the American Novel.*
JUAN FILLOY, *Op Oloop.*
ANDY FITCH, *Pop Poetics.*
GUSTAVE FLAUBERT, *Bouvard and Pécuchet.*
KASS FLEISHER, *Talking out of School.*
FORD MADOX FORD,
　The March of Literature.
JON FOSSE, *Aliss at the Fire.*
　Melancholy.
MAX FRISCH, *I'm Not Stiller.*
　Man in the Holocene.
CARLOS FUENTES, *Christopher Unborn.*
　Distant Relations.
　Terra Nostra.
　Where the Air Is Clear.
TAKEHIKO FUKUNAGA, *Flowers of Grass.*
WILLIAM GADDIS, *J R.*
　The Recognitions.

FOR A FULL LIST OF PUBLICATIONS, VISIT:
www.dalkeyarchive.com

SELECTED DALKEY ARCHIVE TITLES

JANICE GALLOWAY, *Foreign Parts.*
The Trick Is to Keep Breathing.
WILLIAM H. GASS, *Cartesian Sonata and Other Novellas.*
Finding a Form.
A Temple of Texts.
The Tunnel.
Willie Masters' Lonesome Wife.
GÉRARD GAVARRY, *Hoppla! 1 2 3.*
ETIENNE GILSON,
The Arts of the Beautiful.
Forms and Substances in the Arts.
C. S. GISCOMBE, *Giscome Road.*
Here.
DOUGLAS GLOVER, *Bad News of the Heart.*
WITOLD GOMBROWICZ,
A Kind of Testament.
PAULO EMÍLIO SALES GOMES, *P's Three Women.*
GEORGI GOSPODINOV, *Natural Novel.*
JUAN GOYTISOLO, *Count Julian.*
Juan the Landless.
Makbara.
Marks of Identity.
HENRY GREEN, *Back.*
Blindness.
Concluding.
Doting.
Nothing.
JACK GREEN, *Fire the Bastards!*
JIŘÍ GRUŠA, *The Questionnaire.*
MELA HARTWIG, *Am I a Redundant Human Being?*
JOHN HAWKES, *The Passion Artist.*
Whistlejacket.
ELIZABETH HEIGHWAY, ED., *Contemporary Georgian Fiction.*
ALEKSANDAR HEMON, ED.,
Best European Fiction.
AIDAN HIGGINS, *Balcony of Europe.*
Blind Man's Bluff
Bornholm Night-Ferry.
Flotsam and Jetsam.
Langrishe, Go Down.
Scenes from a Receding Past.
KEIZO HINO, *Isle of Dreams.*
KAZUSHI HOSAKA, *Plainsong.*
ALDOUS HUXLEY, *Antic Hay.*
Crome Yellow.
Point Counter Point.
Those Barren Leaves.
Time Must Have a Stop.
NAOYUKI II, *The Shadow of a Blue Cat.*
GERT JONKE, *The Distant Sound.*
Geometric Regional Novel.
Homage to Czerny.
The System of Vienna.
JACQUES JOUET, *Mountain R.*
Savage.
Upstaged.

MIEKO KANAI, *The Word Book.*
YORAM KANIUK, *Life on Sandpaper.*
HUGH KENNER, *Flaubert.*
Joyce and Beckett: The Stoic Comedians.
Joyce's Voices.
DANILO KIŠ, *The Attic.*
Garden, Ashes.
The Lute and the Scars
Psalm 44.
A Tomb for Boris Davidovich.
ANITA KONKKA, *A Fool's Paradise.*
GEORGE KONRÁD, *The City Builder.*
TADEUSZ KONWICKI, *A Minor Apocalypse.*
The Polish Complex.
MENIS KOUMANDAREAS, *Koula.*
ELAINE KRAF, *The Princess of 72nd Street.*
JIM KRUSOE, *Iceland.*
AYŞE KULIN, *Farewell: A Mansion in Occupied Istanbul.*
EMILIO LASCANO TEGUI, *On Elegance While Sleeping.*
ERIC LAURRENT, *Do Not Touch.*
VIOLETTE LEDUC, *La Bâtarde.*
EDOUARD LEVÉ, *Autoportrait.*
Suicide.
MARIO LEVI, *Istanbul Was a Fairy Tale.*
DEBORAH LEVY, *Billy and Girl.*
JOSÉ LEZAMA LIMA, *Paradiso.*
ROSA LIKSOM, *Dark Paradise.*
OSMAN LINS, *Avalovara.*
The Queen of the Prisons of Greece.
ALF MAC LOCHLAINN,
The Corpus in the Library.
Out of Focus.
RON LOEWINSOHN, *Magnetic Field(s).*
MINA LOY, *Stories and Essays of Mina Loy.*
D. KEITH MANO, *Take Five.*
MICHELINE AHARONIAN MARCOM,
The Mirror in the Well.
BEN MARCUS,
The Age of Wire and String.
WALLACE MARKFIELD,
Teitlebaum's Window.
To an Early Grave.
DAVID MARKSON, *Reader's Block.*
Wittgenstein's Mistress.
CAROLE MASO, *AVA.*
LADISLAV MATEJKA AND KRYSTYNA POMORSKA, EDS.,
Readings in Russian Poetics: Formalist and Structuralist Views.
HARRY MATHEWS, *Cigarettes.*
The Conversions.
The Human Country: New and Collected Stories.
The Journalist.
My Life in CIA.
Singular Pleasures.
The Sinking of the Odradek Stadium.
Tlooth.

SELECTED DALKEY ARCHIVE TITLES

JOSEPH McELROY,
  Night Soul and Other Stories.
ABDELWAHAB MEDDEB, *Talismano.*
GERHARD MEIER, *Isle of the Dead.*
HERMAN MELVILLE, *The Confidence-Man.*
AMANDA MICHALOPOULOU, *I'd Like.*
STEVEN MILLHAUSER, *The Barnum Museum.*
  In the Penny Arcade.
RALPH J. MILLS, JR., *Essays on Poetry.*
MOMUS, *The Book of Jokes.*
CHRISTINE MONTALBETTI, *The Origin of Man.*
  Western.
OLIVE MOORE, *Spleen.*
NICHOLAS MOSLEY, *Accident.*
  Assassins.
  Catastrophe Practice.
  Experience and Religion.
  A Garden of Trees.
  Hopeful Monsters.
  Imago Bird.
  Impossible Object.
  Inventing God.
  Judith.
  Look at the Dark.
  Natalie Natalia.
  Serpent.
  Time at War.
WARREN MOTTE,
  *Fables of the Novel: French Fiction
    since 1990.*
  *Fiction Now: The French Novel in
    the 21st Century.*
  *Oulipo: A Primer of Potential
    Literature.*
GERALD MURNANE, *Barley Patch.*
  Inland.
YVES NAVARRE, *Our Share of Time.*
  Sweet Tooth.
DOROTHY NELSON, *In Night's City.*
  Tar and Feathers.
ESHKOL NEVO, *Homesick.*
WILFRIDO D. NOLLEDO, *But for the Lovers.*
FLANN O'BRIEN, *At Swim-Two-Birds.*
  The Best of Myles.
  The Dalkey Archive.
  The Hard Life.
  The Poor Mouth.
  The Third Policeman.
CLAUDE OLLIER, *The Mise-en-Scène.*
  Wert and the Life Without End.
GIOVANNI ORELLI, *Walaschek's Dream.*
PATRIK OUŘEDNÍK, *Europeana.*
  The Opportune Moment, 1855.
BORIS PAHOR, *Necropolis.*
FERNANDO DEL PASO, *News from the
    Empire.*
  Palinuro of Mexico.
ROBERT PINGET, *The Inquisitory.*
  Mahu or The Material.
  Trio.
MANUEL PUIG, *Betrayed by Rita Hayworth.*

The Buenos Aires Affair.
Heartbreak Tango.
RAYMOND QUENEAU, *The Last Days.*
  Odile.
  Pierrot Mon Ami.
  Saint Glinglin.
ANN QUIN, *Berg.*
  Passages.
  Three.
  Triptics.
ISHMAEL REED, *The Free-Lance Pallbearers.*
  The Last Days of Louisiana Red.
  Ishmael Reed: The Plays.
  Juice!
  Reckless Eyeballing.
  The Terrible Threes.
  The Terrible Twos.
  Yellow Back Radio Broke-Down.
JASIA REICHARDT, *15 Journeys Warsaw
    to London.*
NOËLLE REVAZ, *With the Animals.*
JOÃO UBALDO RIBEIRO, *House of the
    Fortunate Buddhas.*
JEAN RICARDOU, *Place Names.*
RAINER MARIA RILKE, *The Notebooks of
    Malte Laurids Brigge.*
JULIÁN RÍOS, *The House of Ulysses.*
  Larva: A Midsummer Night's Babel.
  Poundemonium.
  Procession of Shadows.
AUGUSTO ROA BASTOS, *I the Supreme.*
DANIËL ROBBERECHTS, *Arriving in Avignon.*
JEAN ROLIN, *The Explosion of the
    Radiator Hose.*
OLIVIER ROLIN, *Hotel Crystal.*
ALIX CLEO ROUBAUD, *Alix's Journal.*
JACQUES ROUBAUD, *The Form of a
    City Changes Faster, Alas, Than
    the Human Heart.*
  The Great Fire of London.
  Hortense in Exile.
  Hortense Is Abducted.
  The Loop.
  Mathematics:
  The Plurality of Worlds of Lewis.
  The Princess Hoppy.
  Some Thing Black.
RAYMOND ROUSSEL, *Impressions of Africa.*
VEDRANA RUDAN, *Night.*
STIG SÆTERBAKKEN, *Siamese.*
  Self Control.
LYDIE SALVAYRE, *The Company of Ghosts.*
  The Lecture.
  The Power of Flies.
LUIS RAFAEL SÁNCHEZ,
  Macho Camacho's Beat.
SEVERO SARDUY, *Cobra & Maitreya.*
NATHALIE SARRAUTE,
  Do You Hear Them?
  Martereau.
  The Planetarium.

SELECTED DALKEY ARCHIVE TITLES

ARNO SCHMIDT, *Collected Novellas.*
  Collected Stories.
  Nobodaddy's Children.
  Two Novels.
ASAF SCHURR, *Motti.*
GAIL SCOTT, *My Paris.*
DAMION SEARLS, *What We Were Doing*
  and Where We Were Going.
JUNE AKERS SEESE,
  Is This What Other Women Feel Too?
  What Waiting Really Means.
BERNARD SHARE, *Inish.*
  Transit.
VIKTOR SHKLOVSKY, *Bowstring.*
  Knight's Move.
  A Sentimental Journey:
  Memoirs 1917–1922.
  Energy of Delusion: A Book on Plot.
  Literature and Cinematography.
  Theory of Prose.
  Third Factory.
  Zoo, or Letters Not about Love.
PIERRE SINIAC, *The Collaborators.*
KJERSTI A. SKOMSVOLD, *The Faster I Walk,*
  the Smaller I Am.
JOSEF ŠKVORECKÝ, *The Engineer of*
  Human Souls.
GILBERT SORRENTINO,
  Aberration of Starlight.
  Blue Pastoral.
  Crystal Vision.
  Imaginative Qualities of Actual
  Things.
  Mulligan Stew.
  Pack of Lies.
  Red the Fiend.
  The Sky Changes.
  Something Said.
  Splendide-Hôtel.
  Steelwork.
  Under the Shadow.
W. M. SPACKMAN, *The Complete Fiction.*
ANDRZEJ STASIUK, *Dukla.*
  Fado.
GERTRUDE STEIN, *The Making of Americans.*
  A Novel of Thank You.
LARS SVENDSEN, *A Philosophy of Evil.*
PIOTR SZEWC, *Annihilation.*
GONÇALO M. TAVARES, *Jerusalem.*
  Joseph Walser's Machine.
  Learning to Pray in the Age of
  Technique.
LUCIAN DAN TEODOROVICI,
  Our Circus Presents . . .
NIKANOR TERATOLOGEN, *Assisted Living.*
STEFAN THEMERSON, *Hobson's Island.*
  The Mystery of the Sardine.
  Tom Harris.
TAEKO TOMIOKA, *Building Waves.*

JOHN TOOMEY, *Sleepwalker.*
JEAN-PHILIPPE TOUSSAINT, *The Bathroom.*
  Camera.
  Monsieur.
  Reticence.
  Running Away.
  Self-Portrait Abroad.
  Television.
  The Truth about Marie.
DUMITRU TSEPENEAG, *Hotel Europa.*
  The Necessary Marriage.
  Pigeon Post.
  Vain Art of the Fugue.
ESTHER TUSQUETS, *Stranded.*
DUBRAVKA UGRESIC, *Lend Me Your*
  Character.
  Thank You for Not Reading.
TOR ULVEN, *Replacement.*
MATI UNT, *Brecht at Night.*
  Diary of a Blood Donor.
  Things in the Night.
ÁLVARO URIBE AND OLIVIA SEARS, EDS.,
  Best of Contemporary Mexican Fiction.
ELOY URROZ, *Friction.*
  The Obstacles.
LUISA VALENZUELA, *Dark Desires and*
  the Others.
  He Who Searches.
PAUL VERHAEGHEN, *Omega Minor.*
AGLAJA VETERANYI, *Why the Child Is*
  Cooking in the Polenta.
BORIS VIAN, *Heartsnatcher.*
LLORENÇ VILLALONGA, *The Dolls' Room.*
TOOMAS VINT, *An Unending Landscape.*
ORNELA VORPSI, *The Country Where No*
  One Ever Dies.
AUSTRYN WAINHOUSE, *Hedyphagetica.*
CURTIS WHITE, *America's Magic Mountain.*
  The Idea of Home.
  Memories of My Father Watching TV.
  Requiem.
DIANE WILLIAMS, *Excitability:*
  Selected Stories.
  Romancer Erector.
DOUGLAS WOOLF, *Wall to Wall.*
  Ya! & John-Juan.
JAY WRIGHT, *Polynomials and Pollen.*
  The Presentable Art of Reading
  Absence.
PHILIP WYLIE, *Generation of Vipers.*
MARGUERITE YOUNG, *Angel in the Forest.*
  Miss MacIntosh, My Darling.
REYOUNG, *Unbabbling.*
VLADO ŽABOT, *The Succubus.*
ZORAN ŽIVKOVIĆ, *Hidden Camera.*
LOUIS ZUKOFSKY, *Collected Fiction.*
VITOMIL ZUPAN, *Minuet for Guitar.*
SCOTT ZWIREN, *God Head.*